LUNAR JUSTICE

A SCIENCE FICTION COZY MYSTERY:
A FEELER SERIES (BOOK 3)

KATHERINE OKIA

AGWANG PRESS

First Paperback edition published 2024.

ISBN: 978-1-951722-13-5 Paperback

ISBN: 978-1-951722-12-8 eBook

For my darling daughter, Marta
For my supportive husband, Peter

CONTENTS

CHAPTER 1

Cora and Aunt Ferna emerged from a bland, white tunnel into the waiting area of Lunar City's spaceport. They stepped into a large sprawling area sectioned into four seating areas, bustling with business men, fashionable women, and energetic children criss-crossing the aisles. Although uninteresting gray carpet covered the floor, and beige, gray monotonous murals adorned the walls, nothing compared to the clear open dome that made up the roof. The inky-black night sky dominated the clear-dome only interrupted by tiny points of lights and a memorizing view of the Earth.

For a moment, Cora stood still, partially blocking the other passengers emerging from their shuttle. She peered through the clear dome at the sky above the lunar landscape. On the earth-facing side of the moon, the Earth would be visible at all times. It looked like a blue and white orb against an inky sky. She hadn't been to Lunar City since she was a child, and the site of the clean but busy spaceport gave her a thrill for adventure.

"We should take an excursion since the lunar day will end in about twelve Earth days," Cora said with a broad smile as she continued walking with her aunt. She was smaller than most members of her family, with curly brown hair, bronze skin, and a fit frame. She wore a soft green dress that reached her knees. The dress accompanied practical black shoes and a matching travel bag.

"I'm sure someone will arrange that for you," Aunt Ferna snickered. She was around Cora's height with the same light brown skin. But her aunt was a little rounder with curly gray hair and the beginnings of crow's feet. "I plan to stay inside, where it's warm and safe."

"You've come all the way to the moon," Cora said. "Don't you want to have a pleasant lunar stroll?"

"My dear, I toured several sights on the moon's surface in my twenties," Aunt Ferna said. "I'm more interested in reconnecting with my friends."

They strolled further into one of the seating areas filled with rows of chairs interspersed with small tables. A bored woman in a business jumpsuit casually scrolled through a floating screen while a tired frowning dad chased a toddler desperate for their own adventure, or so Cora thought. The intricate swirls on the wall's murals continued throughout the spaceport's waiting area, but she couldn't take her eyes off the sky for too long. The whole area buzzed with activity, leaving Cora feeling giddy.

"I don't remember the waiting area being this large," Cora said, shouldering her bag. She was a Feeler with the ability to sense other people's emotions. But a crowd this large would overwhelm her mind, so she currently had her shield up in self-defense.

"Yes, my friend Kenna told me the Lunar City council remodeled the spaceport twice," Aunt Ferna said. "They increased the size and comfort level both times. Notice how quiet it is for the number of people."

Cora nodded, absorbing the sight of so many travelers.

"It seems they might need another remodel," Cora said. "People are jostling for space." She paused and turned to Aunt Ferna. "Where do you think we should meet Brian and Benjamin?"

"I'm not sure," Aunt Ferna said, searching the crowd.

"Let's stroll a little," Cora said. "Maybe we'll run into them."

"I'm too old for that much walking," Aunt Ferna groaned. "Maybe we could reach them on our comm bracelets." These bracelets connected her to the High-Frequency Network known as the Net, which allowed communications, business transactions, and purchases with credits or trackable electronic credits.

"Very well," Cora said with a giggle. She reached for her wrist and pressed the button on a white band. This button caused a floating screen to appear above the comm bracelet. She selected a link on her screen and launched a vidchat with Brian. A moment later, his face appeared on the screen.

"There you are," Brian said with a broad smile that made Cora's chest flutter. After investigating and solving the murder of his uncle a year ago, then dealing with a similarly mysterious string of deaths in her friend's family, they had never been closer. "We just arrived. Why don't you walk straight to the antigrav lifts and we'll meet you there?"

In the center of the spaceport, Cora spied two antigrav lifts. They were two clear cylinders that reached from the ground to the top floors of the spaceport's waiting area. An incoming floating train brought passengers to the spaceport's top floor. After they exited the train, they waited in line to take the antigrav lifts to the ground floor, which contained the waiting area to board the next shuttle to Earth.

"Okay, we're close to the lifts," Cora said, closing her floating screen.

She wrapped one arm around Aunt Ferna's arm and helped her amble toward the antigrav lifts.

"You know, aunt, I think you're right," Cora said, watching the trickle of visitors filling the waiting area. "Lunar City's becoming more popular with each passing year."

"I blame the casinos," Aunt Ferna said. "That's what happened to my poor Oliver."

Cora rolled her eyes. Her aunt always blamed other people for her son's bad behavior. She and her aunt could never agree on Oliver Robertson. Aunt Ferna spoiled her only son who was born an Askovian with Feeler abilities, like

Cora's. That made him one of a small percentage of humanity that had developed special abilities. Some examples included Readers who could detect one's thoughts or Movers who could manipulate objects with their minds. Oliver's Feeler abilities allowed him to sense others' emotional state, but also he could manipulate their feelings. Oliver used his abilities to hurt those around him. Cora hated him.

They reached the lifts, and a moment later, she spotted Brian and increased her pace toward him. He had piercing blue-gray eyes and jet black hair. Although averaged height, he was quite athletic. As Cora reached him, she let go of Aunt Ferna's arm and stopped half a meter away from him.

"I'm so happy to finally see you," Cora said with a warm smile. "It's been a long four months. How've you been?"

Brian closed the gap between them and gave her a long, comforting hug, and she melted into his arms. Something about this just felt so right. She could stay here in his arms forever.

"All right, time to break it up," Benjamin said with glee. "He wore a casual jumpsuit with bright colors. Cora had never seen him in casual clothes before. As Brian's father, he looked like an older, usually well-dressed version of Brian with the same piercing blue eyes, but where Brian had jet black hair, his hair was graying.

"Benjamin," Cora said, letting go of Brian and giving his dad a quick hug. "How've you been? How's retirement in Lunar City?"

"Retirement suits me perfectly," Benjamin said with a sly smile. "This is the first time in maybe two decades I've truly been able to enjoy myself. I've explored the caves and mountains on the moon, played in the casino, and even explored the Originals Dome."

"What are Originals?" Cora asked.

"Maybe we could start making our way out of here?" Aunt Ferna grumbled. "My feet are aching."

Benjamin hugged Aunt Ferna.

"And how've you been, old thing?" Benjamin chuckled. "Maybe it's time for you to get replacement feet if they're bothering you that much."

"Old! Who're you calling old?" Aunt Ferna said with a half-smile. "By the way, where are we staying?"

Just then, a high-pitched scream cut through the air, ending everybody's conversation.

"Aria, Aria, what's happening?" a woman in a coral dress cried. Running back and forth on the same floor at Cora, she skirted one of the lift's tubes with raised hands, while turning up to a lift stuck between floors. "Somebody help her, please."

Cora turned and looked in the same direction as the woman in a coral dress. She spotted a young lady with long straight brown hair, banging on the clear walls of the antigrav lift and screaming in anguish. Her lift car had paused halfway down, and Cora wondered if the woman was panicking because of the immobile lift. In any case, Cora couldn't hear her and guessed the lift must be soundproofed. A glance at the second lift's car showed her it had stopped on the top floor where it stood, empty.

She quickly checked her shield, making sure it still kept her safe, as sometimes a shock made her forget to maintain it. If she lowered her shield, the large throng and the anguish of the poor girl would overwhelm her. After several seconds of pounding, she collapsed to the floor and stopped moving.

"Aria, talk to me. What's happening?" the coral-dress woman called repeatedly, leaning against the lift's tube as if trying to push her way in. "Somebody help!"

A moment later, three Interplanetary Security or IPS agents ran to the antigrav lifts. The IPS was supposed to serve as the police force for any human colony or city outside Earth. A short, bald male agent directed the crowd to step away from the lifts. A black-haired female agent operated the lift's controls, forcing both lifts to the ground floor.

The coral-dress woman tried to shove past the black-haired female agent. But an athletic red-haired male agent stepped forward, held her and forced her further away from the lift. A tall, blond, athletic man put his arms around the woman while she cried and continued calling for Aria. After a quick inspection, the black-haired IPS agent pressed the button on her comm bracelet, which resulted in the spaceport's lock down.

It looked like Cora would not be going anywhere just yet. Passengers couldn't use the lifts to enter or exit the waiting area. A hoard of other IPS agents arrived. One of them pushed a floating medipad, a device that could expand to create a hospital bed, extend probes to correct medical injuries, and resuscitate unconscious victims. Once they'd forced the doors open, they connected it to the woman in the antigrav lift. It took less than a minute for the black-haired agent to shake her head. The woman in the coral dress continued weeping.

Cora watched the scene unfold with a pang. She wished she could help and also knew anything she said or did wouldn't be appreciated.

"Attention, attention everyone," the black-haired IPS agent said as the waiting area became quiet. "I'm Agent Taylor. Please cooperate with the IPS agents and provide your contact information and any knowledge you have about this death."

As the noise of chatter and distress picked back up, the IPS agents fanned through the crowd and began questioning passengers. Agent Taylor stayed with the crying coral-dress woman and the blond man.

About an hour later, the IPS agents had gathered their identifications and their hotel information. Cora, Aunt Ferna, Benjamin, and Brian waited for the IPS's permission to leave the spaceport.

"I think I recognize the deceased," Aunt Ferna said with a frown. "It was Myrtle's eldest daughter. Oh, what's her name... Aria. I think that's Jane, the younger one." She pointed to the crying woman. "They're Spencers, but not the rich side of the family, although they're all powerful Readers."

"I think I met Myrtle at one of the Spencer tea parties," Cora said in a low voice. "I feel so sorry for her. I wish I could help."

"It's so sad," Aunt Ferna said. "Myrtle will be devastated. I'll call on them and give my condolences."

"Do you know the gentleman next to her?" Cora asked.

"He's one of the Yarmouths," Aunt Ferna said. "But I'm not sure which one; they had four boys."

"How is it you know everyone?" Benjamin asked, trying to lighten the mood.

"I'm going to speak to them," Aunt Ferna said, ignoring Benjamin. "Maybe I can help. Come with me, dear."

"Aunt, I don't think this is a good idea," Cora said as her aunt wrapped an arm around hers and dragged her toward Jane.

A moment later, they stood near Jane, who was still shedding quiet tears on the blond-haired man's shoulders. He looked up and glared as they drew near.

"What do you want?" he asked.

"My dear, you don't know me," Aunt Ferna said. "My name is Ferna Robertson, and Myrtle Spencer is a close friend. I've known Aria and Jane since they were children. Please let me know if there's anything I can do to help."

The blond-haired man's face softened, and Jane wiped her eyes, turning to Aunt Ferna.

"It's alright Drew. I remember Aunt Ferna," Jane said in a watery voice. "Thank you for offering, but I've already contacted my parents. I'll be fine when they get here." She turned to Cora. "Do I know you?"

"I don't think so," Cora said, a little taken aback. "I don't think we've met."

"No, we've never met," Jane said with wide eyes. "But you helped solve that murder with the Pendleton family a few months ago."

Cora shifted from foot-to-foot, unused to the attention.

"I don't think this is the time for that," Drew said in a Lunar City drawl.

"Of course, you're right," Jane said in a quiet voice. "But is there any chance you can help us find out what happened to Aria?"

"No, I'm sorry," Cora said in a gentle voice. "I'm on vacation here and I don't want to get involved in another murder."

"What makes you think it's a murder?" Brian asked, a little agitated.

Cora jumped. She hadn't realized he was standing beside her.

"Aria just dropped dead, and she doesn't seem injured," Cora said.

"It could've been a disease or some genetic defect," Brian said in an irritated tone.

"You're right," Cora said, confused by Brian's troubled face.

"Pardon me, I'm Agent Taylor," she said, turning to Aunt Ferna, Cora, Benjamin, and Brian. "I'd like to request that you not talk to the family at this time. Maybe you can continue this conversation tomorrow."

"Yes, I'll call on Myrtle tomorrow," Aunt Ferna said as the four of them turned to leave.

"So, tell me about our hotel, Athos Tower?" Cora asked.

"We opted for a touch of luxury. Each floor is an entire suite," Benjamin said. "Ours has four bedrooms, each with a private bathroom. It's perfect—I know you'll enjoy it.

What's upsetting Brian so much? Cora thought.

CHAPTER 2

Cora followed Aunt Ferna, Brian, and Benjamin down a wide corridor leading to the end of the ground floor of the spaceport. Only a handful of people passed them, heading in the same direction. Cora lowered her shield in tiny increments, trying to understand how others felt after the tragedy.

"Am I missing something?" Cora asked. "There are people passing us and I can't sense most of them—only the occasional person."

"I would say Lunar City is a low trust society," Benjamin said, going into his familiar lecture mode. "Most Originals here wear neurowalls. There are also special ones for Askovs with no abilities and Askovians who can't shield their minds to defend themselves."

Neurowalls stopped the wearer's emotions and thoughts from transmitting outside of their minds. They also acted as a shield to prevent other Askovians from manipulating the wearer's emotions or thoughts.

"What are Originals?" Cora asked. "You've used that term twice."

"Oh that," Benjamin said with a chuckle. "They're really non-Askovs, but they don't like that term. They consider themselves the *original* humans, so they called themselves Originals, implying, of course, that we are not actually human anymore."

"I think that's a bit of an oversimplification," Brian said in a serious tone. "What has actually happened is the non-Askov humans living here have less political power than Askovs and Askovians. For example, Askovs fill the Lunar City council, which doesn't operate like other Earth governments. After a lot of protests, they added one Original, who basically has no power."

"Well, I hate to say this, but Originals have a point," Aunt Ferna said. "There's plenty of evidence of our genetic differences."

"It doesn't mean they shouldn't have access to Lunar City's political power," Brian said. "The Originals continue to differentiate themselves from us as they sense they're losing political ground. It won't end well."

The four of them lapsed into silence as they reached the lifts to take them floor below ground, where a floating train would ferry them to Lunar City. As the trains approach the spaceport, they deposit passengers heading to Earth on the upper level. Then they transition via tunnel to the lower level to transport visitors to Lunar City.

"On a different note, I've always wondered why anyone would consent to having hardware like a neurowall attached to their body," Cora said. "Seems like a new type of prison."

"Well, a gamer might have permanent gamer glasses attached to their eyes," Brian said with a thoughtful expression. "We've had cousins that did that."

"And that's what I mean," Cora said. "Even though the tech is removable, most never take it out. So, they spend the rest of their lives with augmented vision. It's another type of prison."

"I understand what you're saying," Benjamin said. "But Lunar City is Earth's wild frontier. The IPS has records of many Readers harming mostly Originals but sometimes Askovs, and they've done nothing about it. I think Oliver was the only Feeler to have crossed the line, but the IPS's response was the same—nothing. Everyone who wears a neurowall feels they need protection from intrusive Askovian abilities."

"Also, our cousin was a teen," Brian said. "I don't think too many adults would consent to do tech augmentation unless they were here in Lunar City."

"You'd be surprised," Aunt Ferna said. "I have friends, older than me, who have gamer glasses attached to their eyes. They don't want the bother of removing the attachments. My friends consider it fashionable to have tech attachments."

Many people passed them, and Cora, on reflex, raised her shield. She thought she saw Stephen Marsh. As she turned and looked through the crowd, she realized she'd made a mistake. Steven was a hacker who, for the most part, stayed on the legal side of the law, but he had helped Oliver murder her sister. It turned out Oliver had manipulated him, but the EGS still wanted to arrest him. EGS stood for Earth Global Security and provided the police force for Earth, investigating crimes and enforcing laws.

The EGS works with the IPS, making it dangerous for Steven, so that couldn't be him, she thought.

As they reached the end of the wide corridor, they took the large antigrav lift down one flight and emerged onto an underground platform. A floating train waited for passengers, and the four boarded the train. It left the station about five minutes later. The inside of their train car was clean and white, like the spaceport. It had a bank of windows on both sides, which allowed them to see the surrounding tunnel walls as the train sped through. A handful of people joined them in their car, and she noticed more than once that they glanced at her. When she returned their gaze, they looked away.

"Tell me I'm imagining this," Cora said in a loud whisper. "That couple is staring at me."

"They probably are, my dear," Benjamin said. "There are Originals, and they're frightened of you."

"Of me?" Cora asked with raised eyebrows. "Why?"

"It's the database," Brian said. "The Originals have a database of all Askovs and Askovians. It's somehow updated as soon as any of us set foot in the spaceport."

"By now they know you're a Feeler," Benjamin said. "They know you can sense emotions and possibly manipulate them as well. Even though they quickly gather our information, there're many mistakes in their database."

Something about being part of a database made Cora shiver.

She glanced at the peeking couple and turned to Aunt Ferna.

"I think we are in more danger from them," Cora said. "Especially if their database has mistakes. Did you know about this?"

"Some of it, yes," Aunt Ferna said, shaking her head. "It's sad that relations between the Originals and Askovs have deteriorated. My friend Kenna told me about Lunar City politics. It looks as if they'll get a little worse."

"Why?" Cora asked.

"There's some political stuff coming up," Aunt Ferna said, rolling her eyes with a hand wave. "I haven't taken the time to understand it. It's something to do with the way the council is structured."

"I just wanted to have a relaxing vacation," Cora said with a sigh.

Brian grasped her hand and gave it a gentle squeeze, and her tension drained away.

About an hour later, they reached Lunar City. Cora's tingle of excitement returned as she stepped onto the floating train's platform filled with passengers going to other parts of Lunar City. Images of the casinos, Central Park, cave adventures, and more interrupted the depot's sparkling white walls. She squeezed Brian's hand, gazing at the images, which were subtle advertisements to encourage tourism. A broad smile covered her face as she planned future adventures.

They followed the crowd to the antigrav lift. A moment later, they stood inside Lunar City's main dome at the edge of a busy pathway, with people crossing in both directions. A beautiful park lay on the other side of the walkway, and a giant building stood behind them.

"This is Athos Tower," Benjamin said with a grand wave. "We're staying on the eleventh floor. Come, I've got a surprise for you." A sly grin covered his face.

"Does the park have a name?" Cora asked, peering at the dense vegetation.

"Central Park," Brian chuckled as he wrapped an arm around Cora. "Come."

The four of them strolled to the double doors of the building and stepped into the lobby. It reminded Cora of Tymal with one wall covered in faux light wood slats. Most wood on the moon was manufactured, as it was too expensive to transport. The lobby also displayed several potted plants scattered throughout, which created a warm and cozy atmosphere.

They passed two padded benches as they made their way to the antigrav lift and, a moment later, stepped out onto the eleventh floor. Cora gaped at the off-white walls interspersed with images from the moon's landscape and the plush gray carpet. Once they reached the door to their suite, it slid open with a whoosh. Cora grinned.

"Omar, I haven't seen you in months," Cora said, stepping to the older man for a hug. "How have you been?" She met Omar about a year ago while she investigated her sister's murder. She liked his down-to-Earth nature and enjoyed talking to him.

"I'm old, but I'm still moving," Omar said with a chuckle. He was a tall, thin man with wrinkled brown skin and a cloud of white hair. "Let me introduce you to my girlfriend, Irene."

"Hello," Irene said with a nod. She was an older lady, a little plump, with white hair and a very kind smile. Cora could see what attracted Omar.

"Come in," Benjamin said, making his way to the dining table. "Have a snack. We've a wide variety of options here."

The whole group made their way past the living room and toward the dining room. The small and functional living room contained a gray and white sofa with a low, light wood coffee table and opposite were two gray over-stuffed chairs with white print flowers.

Cora gazed around the room and spotted a wall full of beautiful garden images from Earth. She also glanced at the five doors leading from the room. Only one was open, which led to the bathroom. The other four must've been their bedrooms.

"We heard about Aria Spencer's passing," Omar said, taking a bite of an apricot cookie. "I only met her in passing, but her parents must be devastated."

"I know. I'm going to visit Myrtle tomorrow and see what I can do to help," Aunt Ferna said in a solemn tone and swallowed some tea.

"I know it's early, but does the IPS have any idea what happened to the poor girl?" Irene asked and munched on the last of a small cook-ie.

"No, we've been wondering that ourselves," Benjamin said. "What can cause screaming in pain and sudden death?"

Cora shook her head as her mind had gone over the same thoughts.

"I hope they figure it out soon, so the family has a little peace," Brian said, frowning. "I remember what it was like when Uncle Harold passed." Harold Albright used to run the Albright Corporation, which provided mining management to several small mines, including Cora's.

Benjamin cleared his throat.

Cora sensed his discomfort at the discussion of Harold's death.

"Oh, I nearly forgot," Benjamin said around a mouth full of cookie. "We're required to give you a quick orientation about this suite." He swallowed the last of his cookie and took a sip of tea. "Safety, you know. First, there is the front door."

Everyone chortled.

"You obviously know how to get in and out that way," Benjamin said, leaning back in his chair and going a little into lecture mode like a professor. "But there are other ways to escape in an emergency like fire." Every bedroom has an airlock—this hotel used to be a spaceship. It could be a little hidden, but it lets you out of the room. The portal leads to a ladder you can take all the way to the first floor. Then, you can exit the building quickly.

"Yes, professor," Omar said, snickering. Ironically, Omar had been Benjamin's teacher years ago in Tymal.

"If, for some reason, the meal crafter doesn't work, you can go to the pantry," Benjamin said, pointing at a blank wall near the table. The crafter prepared meals in a pantry, transformed them into energy, transported them to the table, and reassembled them into the original meal. "We can open the pantry and check for blockages. Also, the bathroom has its own robot that can fix any issues that might come up. We can always call management if we can't correct something."

"Anything else?" Cora asked, downing the last of her coffee.

"No, that's it," Benjamin said, eyeing the menu on the meal crafter. "Now let's go back to stuffing our faces."

Everybody cheered, and they caught up on the news from Earth. Benjamin filled them in on the news from Lunar City. But Brian reached out for Cora's hand under the table and gave her a gentle squeeze. A warm, comforting feeling spread through her chest—as if she was at home.

CHAPTER 3

Cora and Brian sat at the dining room table of their suite, each sipping a cup of coffee and munching on a strawberry and blueberry scone for breakfast. They were catching up on the four months they'd been apart. Cora brushed the crumbs off of her pale-yellow shirt and shook out her sage green pants.

"The number of players is increasing at a very steady rate," Cora said with a broad grin. She loved talking about her game Mystery Adventures, which provided a series of science or math puzzles, allowing gamers to advance to the next level or gain access to special tools. She'd coded it over the last few years, and four months ago she organized a soft launch of her game. "New players have accepted the fee, and I grandfathered in the first gamers."

"I can understand players sticking to your game and even attracting others," Brian said with a chuckle. "I've played Mystery Adventures for hours before, and it's very addicting. Once you solve one puzzle, you become inspired to solve the next."

"What types of new clients did you find here in Lunar City?" she asked.

"Surprisingly, most of them have business in Anteros on Mars," he said, taking a sip of coffee. "This city is only an outpost. The real issue with Lunar City is Spencer Industries dominates most business. It's very difficult to get a foothold here. But Spencer Industries still needs help to distribute raw materials, maintain machinery, and correct supply chain issues. So, there're a lot of auxiliary businesses that help them. My clients take part in the periphery, but they can't compete in the mining business."

"That's interesting." Cora was the sole owner of Brimble Mining and always paid attention to changes in the industry to ensure her company continued to profit. "What about auxiliary businesses for more remote mines like mine on Ganymede?"

"Remote mines don't have enough auxiliary business to support another company," Brian said with eyebrows furrowed. "You'd need a minimum of two to five mines in close proximity to attract other companies who'd be willing to assist with some of the peripheral mining tasks and take on some of the risk."

"But if there were two or five mines in the same location on Ganymede, there'd be no profit," she said with a sigh. "I don't like how vulnerable Brimble Mining is right now."

"Actually, the mines on Mar's moons are almost in the same predicament as yours," he said. "They're not as remote, but much more difficult to get to than the mines on Mars itself."

Cora gave him a shrug of acknowledgement and took another bite from her scone.

"You should be grateful," he said with a frown. "If your mine had been in a better location, it'd be a prime target for a mine jump. That's what started the issue with the Pendleton family." More than a year ago, Spencer Industries had stolen a mine on one of Mars's moons from Pendleton Mining.

"Okay, enough mining talk," she said, taking a sip of coffee. "What else is happening?"

"In about three weeks, my dad is continuing to Mars," he said. "I'm thinking about joining him."

Cora placed her coffee cup on the table with a snap and focused on Brian's words.

"I'm sorry," he said with a sigh. "I should've told you earlier, but right now, I'm only thinking about it."

"How long have you been thinking about it?" she asked in a tight voice.

"About a month," he said with a frown. "For the first time in years, I've been able to spend time with my dad when we've both had easy schedules. I only have nine clients, and dad is fully retired. It's been so nice getting to know him again. I don't want to miss out on that."

"I understand," Cora said in a small voice. "You should spend time with your dad. How long will you be gone?"

"Three or four years," Brian said. "But it'll go by quickly. I mean, you and I have known each other for three years already and that time went by fast."

"I wish I could go with you," she said with a sigh. "But I can't leave Tymal right now. Brimble mining is attached to the Albright Corp, which is headquartered there. That's my family's primary livelihood."

"Your family is you and Aunt Ferna," he said with a lopsided grin. "The two of you could tag along."

"The mine also supports a host of distant relatives," she said. "Also, my game is growing, and it's based in Tymal. I've started getting players, and I even communicate with them periodically. It's been so much fun. I feel as if my life is finally going the way I want, and I don't want to leave it all behind."

Her eyes began to swim with tears, and she wiped them before he noticed.

"I'm sorry, Cora," he said in a low voice. "I feel so torn, but I have a chance for a great relationship with my father or with you. The time I have with my father won't be too long. Also, he's not coming back from Mars. This is a permanent move for my dad and Omar."

Cora gazed at him, nonplussed.

"Does your mom know?" she asked.

"I don't think so," he said. "But I learned a long time ago not to interfere with my parent's marriage. It can get very nasty. After the way Mom treated Dad, though, I don't have that much sympathy for her. So, I've decided to stay out of it, but I really don't want to leave you behind."

Brian reached out for her hand and squeezed it.

"As a compromise, I could move to Lunar City," Cora said. "That way, you'd still have access to clientele needing help with Martian law. Also, I could easily take the shuttle down to Earth for the quarterly meetings with Albright. I'd still have easy access to my customers."

"It's a possibility. I'll think about it," Brian said. "But just to let you know, I'm leaning toward going with my dad."

Cora nodded and looked down at her breakfast. It looked dry and bland now. She'd lost her appetite.

A knock at the door interrupted Cora and Brian's conversation.

"Jane Spencer and Drew Yarmouth at the door for Cora Brimble," the suite's AI said. "Should I let them in?"

Cora and Brian exchanged glances. He shrugged.

"Yes, please let them in," Cora said, turning to the front door.

"Good morning. I'm Jane Spencer," she said, striding into the room in a plain white formal shirt and black slacks. In her mid-twenties, she looked like a younger, more beautiful version of her cousin, Jessica Spencer, with straight shoulder-length brown hair and a no-nonsense look about her. Unlike the day Cora had arrived, she looked put together and calm, but Cora could sense the grief roiling under the surface. "I hope we're not interrupting."

"Morning. Drew Yarmouth," the man said in a strong Lunar City drawl. He followed her into the room looking like a tall, muscular, blond-headed thunder god from an ancient religion.

Cora knew of Jane and Drew's families but had never met them. They were Askovian, and in Jane's family their abilities made them Readers who could discern the thoughts of people around them. Drew's family comprised Movers who could manipulate objects with their minds.

The last time Cora had seen them was in the spaceport, when Aria died. Cora sensed their yawning chasms of hurt, anger, and despair. She considered raising her shield in case their emotions overwhelmed her.

"Cora Brimble?" Jane said with a tense face and a milder Lunar City accent.

Askovs were the family members of the Askovians. Askovs didn't have special abilities, but they produced offspring with special abilities.

One example was Aunt Ferna, who had no abilities but had passed them onto Oliver.

Many Askov parents practiced DNA selection, which resulted in the society's ideal for beautiful children. Jane and Drew had the telltale beautiful faces, flawless skin, thick hair, and trim bodies of the practice. Cora's parents and her Aunt Ferna had genetically edited her sister Sophia and her cousin Oliver. They were both tall, with bronze skin, green eyes, and thick wavy hair. But Cora's parents hadn't bothered selecting the best traits when she was conceived. Instead, she was short, with brown eyes and unruly curly hair. She loved the way she looked, but wondered why her parents had made a different decision about her conception.

Cora nodded, climbing to her feet, followed by Brian. "I'm Brian Farris," he said.

"How can I help you?" Cora said and gestured to a seat.

Jane and Drew nodded and took their seats.

"Would you like something to drink? Coffee? Tea?" Brian asked.

Jane and Drew shook their heads.

"I don't have much time, so I'd like to get to the point," Jane said. "It's been only a day since my sister, Aria, passed away."

"My condolences," Cora said in a quiet voice.

"So, sorry for your loss," Brian said.

"Thank you," Jane said. "I've heard the rumors about you, and I know you're able to find criminals. I'd like to hire you to find out what really happened to my sister Aria."

"No, I can't accept any credits from you," Cora said, raising both hands. "Also, finding criminals is very dangerous. The last two times I tracked a criminal, I nearly died. They attacked me, and I thought I was going to die."

"The IPS asked a few questions yesterday," Jane said in an intense voice. "They feel a Reader killed my sister because other crimes like this have happened, especially on the casino side of Lunar City. I agree with them." Her eyes flickered toward Brian and back. "Would you poke around in one or two casinos...?"

"No!" Brian turned from Cora to Jane. "That's too dangerous. You may not know this, but her cousin used to frequent the casinos, and even he needed to flee for his own safety."

"I'm well aware of Oliver Robertson," Jane said, as her lips formed a line.

Cora caught Jane's subtle finger movements some Readers used to focus their abilities. She felt Jane's mind trying to push on hers and raised her shield in self-defense. Readers were notorious for mind intrusions without permission. When Readers were babies, experiencing their parent's minds was the same as knowing what they were thinking. There were no boundaries. As they matured, their parents typically taught them to respect other's minds, but Cora had witnessed firsthand it was not always the case. Her attendance at Heliton Academy with undisciplined Readers had taught her to shield herself quickly. Before she shielded herself, she felt Jane's deep wells of sadness tinged with raw anger.

"I don't want Cora to go there and borrow credits or even play any games," she continued. "My plan is you could use your Feeler abilities and see if you come across anybody... strange?"

"Let me stop you right there," Cora said, amused by how little Jane knew of her ability. "In Tymal, it's considered rude to invade somebody's mind without their permission. Please remove yourself from Brian's."

Drew chuckled.

Turning pink, Jane shifted in her seat.

"What?" Brian said with raised eyebrows. "Is that what she did?"

"It's considered rude here also," Drew said with a broad grin. "Jane never cared about Reader etiquette. Aria used to lecture her about it, but Jane never stopped."

"I'm sorry," Jane said in a low voice. "I want your help, and I don't want to offend you."

"Next, my Feeler ability doesn't work like that," Cora said, leaning onto the table. "I would need to engage with someone. I would have to hold a conversation or play a casino game. But even then, I can't do that in a crowd. I'd become overwhelmed."

"But Oliver managed it," Jane said.

"And he was much more advanced than I'll ever be," Cora said matter-of-factly.

"But you defeated him. He went to prison," Jane said.

"I was desperate and lucky," Cora said. "As for Aria, I think we should wait for the IPS death report."

"I think you have a good point," Drew said in a firm voice. "Let's wait to see what the IPS has to say."

"Please, don't dismiss me," Jane said in a pleading voice, the no-nonsense air about her deflating all at once. "Something horrible happened to my sister, and I can't let the killer get away with that."

Cora felt a pang of guilt for telling Jane she didn't want to be involved.

"I understand how you feel," Cora said in a softer tone. "But if somebody killed Aria, they won't want to be found and will kill again to protect themselves. This case is very dangerous."

"Aria was my older sister," Jane said, undeterred. "She and Drew were going to be married later this year. We've all known each other since we were kids. Aria was the sweetest sister when we were growing up. She became a music composer and teacher. I can't imagine who'd want to harm her."

"The problem with the IPS is they're not impartial," Drew said. "Instead, they're very sympathetic to the Originals and in the past have ignored issues that the Originals have caused. But it still won't hurt to wait for their report and glean any clues from it."

"The day Aria passed, she was running late," Jane said with a tinge of desperation. "Drew and I went to the spaceport to meet her. Aria and Drew were going on vacation, and I went to see her off. I never thought..." She trailed off and looked at her hands in her lap, eyes watering. When she looked back up, she met Cora's gaze with desperation. "Please, you have to help us," she tried one more time.

"I'm sorry for the loss of your sister," Cora said in a gentle voice. She didn't need to feel the ache in Jane to know it was there, and that Cora's refusal was only making it worse. "How about this?" she suggested. "Let's wait for the IPS report and talk again after."

Cora watched Jane smile in relief, wondering if she'd just signed herself up for trouble.

CHAPTER 4

"How long before we reach Apenninus mountain range?" Cora asked, sitting on an underground floating train from Lunar City to one of Spencer Industries' mines. She wore a white top and pants meant as underclothes for a spacesuit. The outfit covered her entire body, from her white boots to her neck. Her face and hands were still free, though.

"It'll be about thirty minutes to Spencer Industries," Brian said, sitting next to her on the train. He wore a similar white top and pants outfit. "I'm less sure about the hike to the base of the Apenninus."

Originals filled about half of the seats on the train. None of them sat in the row with Cora and Brian, and they also left the rows in front and behind them empty. At this time of the day, many Originals took the train to work as technicians. These jobs included monitoring, maintaining, and updating mining equipment. Cora had read about the mining activities of Spencer industries to learn how to run her mine on Ganymede.

She did her best to ignore the Original's subtle peeking, but it made her shift uncomfortably in her seat. Brian grasped her hand and gave it a gentle squeeze. This was the fourth day of her visit, and she'd hoped they'd get used to her, but they still seemed just as fearful.

"Looks like we're here," he said, standing as the train slowed to a stop.

"I'm so happy to get off this train," she said in a low voice.

They stepped onto the platform and walked to the exit. They each held a small but medium-weight case. The cases held their compacted spacesuits, food, water, and a tent for airless camping.

As they exited the platform, they stepped into the Spencer Industries' dome. Five security rows stood across from them, filling with Originals going to work. They streamed through the security rows, which turned green as each technician passed.

Brian and Cora turned right and followed a short corridor to an airlock.

"Where are the dressing rooms?" Cora asked, glancing around.

"We're going to put the spacesuits over our clothes," Brian said with a chuckle. "We don't need dressing rooms." He gestured to a nearby wall. "Let's change closer to the wall so we don't block anyone."

They placed their cases flat on the floor next to the wall.

"Press this button, and take a step back," he said. "Sometimes it expands a little too vigorously."

Brian selected his button first and a soft white faux silk spacesuit erupted from the side of his case. Cora copied him, but didn't step back far enough and the suit bumped into her feet.

"Oh," she said. "It didn't hurt. I'm just surprised." She replied in response to his concerned face.

Cora sorted through the soft fabric, looking for the pants with foot attachments. She stood and slipped them over her boots and legs, tightening them at the waist. She added a belt with one control button around her waist. Then she slipped on the shirt with glove attachments, leaving the gloves unattached for now. Instead, she attached the top to the belt.

"You look like you're not properly dressed for a ball," she chortled as she looked at Brian. "It's the right material, but it's draped so carelessly over your body."

"I hope you realize you don't look any better," he said with a smirk.

A transparent, soft, gauzy material served as her helmet, which she placed over her head. She attached the head cover to her top and at last attached her gloves.

"Ready?" he asked.

She nodded and pressed the button on the belt of her spacesuit. The soft material instantly hardened, becoming air tight. It remained flexible at the wrists, elbows, neck, knees and hips. A moment later, she heard the steady whoosh of air in her suit. She turned to Brian, who gave her a thumbs up.

"Can you hear me?" he asked.

"Loud and clear," she said with a grin. "Let's get started."

They both collected their cases and stepped through the inner airlock and into the chamber, which opened with a heavy clunk and a whoosh of air. It then slid closed behind them, and an alarm sounded, letting them know that the outer airlock was going to open in ten seconds. Once the alarm stopped, the outer airlock clunked and also opened with a whoosh of air.

A broad smile spread over Cora's face as she took her first steps onto the lunar landscape. She stumbled for a moment as her boots adjusted to Lunar gravity. Alythium lined the floor of the domes, train tunnels, and all antigrav machines. This crystal, found on the moons of several planets, was a key component in maintaining and manipulating localized gravity. It gave Lunar City the same gravity as Earth. But outside on the bare ground, she experienced the Moon's actual gravity.

"This is the first time I've stepped on lunar soil," Cora said with a wobbly step. Fortunately, their cases floated on the moon's surface now that they weren't inside a dome.

"Go slowly," Brian said, concerned as he followed.

After a few minutes of walking, Cora paused and took in the eerie, airless landscape. The light level was like Earth on an overcast day. The blue and white Earth dominated the pitch-black sky. She continued and with each step increased her stride, feeling more confident.

"I thought you might enjoy the hike," he said. "I've been dying to try hiking here and haven't found the time."

"Which way are we going?" she asked.

"Veer left," he said, pointing at the largest structure. "That is the Apenninus mountain range. It's too large to make it all the way to the top, but I thought we might be able to make it to the first foothill, open a tent, and have a little snack before heading back down."

"Sounds excellent," she said, ambling in the mountain's direction. After several steps, she realized she'd stepped along a worn path. "This place must be popular. Not only is there a path to the mountain range, but there are trails heading several other directions as well."

"Yeah, this is a popular tourist destination," he said. "There're several other rock formations to explore here. We're only going to the Apenninus today, but we can come back and explore more."

Cora meandered over the half-buried pebbles on the path. She even found a little foot bridge where a meteorite had dug out a small trench across their path, and somebody else had filled in the missing path with stones. She wished she could hear outside of her suit, instead she heard her own steady breathing as her suit recycled the air.

After thirty minutes, they reached a tiny hill, and they had a slow climb to the top over an unstable pebble surface. They stopped several times to survey the landscape.

At the top, Cora turned and gazed back in the direction they'd come. She saw the dome that contained one of many Spencer Industries mining operations.

"Is that rock art?" she asked, pointing to a large arc of light-colored rocks. Darker sedimentary rocks filled in the arc. "It looks as if it could topple at any moment. Someone must've taken a lot of time to create a stable arrangement."

"Unfortunately," he said, taking in the view. "With so many criss-crossed trails, there's no telling where the rock artist came from."

"Next time, I want to go to the rock art. It looks fascinating."

"I've been meaning to visit those as well. We won't have time today, but let's make a plan to visit in the four weeks that you're going to be here."

"Is that even possible?" she asked, turning to him. "What if you leave in three weeks?"

"Let's not think about that now," he said, reaching for her hand even though they couldn't touch. "We should keep going."

"Yeah, it looks like we have another thirty minutes before we reach the first plateau," she said.

Brian nodded, heading up the steep side of the Apenninus mountain range.

Cora and Brian made the hike without too much trouble due to the lowered gravity. They reached the plateau and Cora chuckled as she looked over the moon's landscape.

"This is amazing," she said with a tiny squeal. "I can't believe I haven't been here before."

"I'm still kicking myself for waiting so long to come here," he said.

Turning to the plateau, Cora spied the uneven ground criss-crossed with cracks and fissures. She also saw the remnants of an avalanche on the far end of the plateau.

"I think we should stay away from that end," Cora said, pointing to the avalanche.

"Definitely," Brian said. "How about here?" He pointed to a flat, smooth area about six meters from the edge of the plateau.

With Brian's instruction, they put their cases together and connected them. He pressed a series of controls on the case, and they both took several steps back.

A moment later, the cases formed a four-by-four meter platform that locked to the ground, engaging its anti-gravity. Next, a white, willowy cloth-like material emerged from the edges of the platform. It grew larger, forming a white dome. They took several more steps away as the dome formed. When it completed inflating, it was about two meters high. A transparent door appeared on one side, facing Cora and Brian.

Cora couldn't help bouncing on her heels with excitement.

"I've never been camping on the moon," she chortled. "This is so exciting. I'm even willing to sacrifice my coffee for hot tea and whatever snacks you brought."

Brian laughed, taking steps toward the transparent door. He disconnected the latches, which released the door with a whoosh of air. He stepped through and Cora followed. An alarm sounded, letting them know that the outer door was not connected. Brian worked to reconnect the outer door's latches while Cora ran her hands over the walls of their chamber. She admired the beautiful engineering that allowed all the surfaces to harden.

"This is amazing material," she said with wonder. "Before it's used, it's soft as silk and when activated becomes hard as metal."

After the transparent door reconnected, the alarm stopped. They worked together to disconnect the inner door's latches. Once opened, Cora and Brian stepped through, resealing the inner door.

"Inflatable chairs and table," she strode to the collection and knocked on the table. "Hard as metal." She turned to him. "What's the tent using for power again?"

"It's an energy saver," he said, reaching for his helmet and peeling it off. "It's light and doesn't take much room, but it'll only last for about forty-eight hours."

Cora removed her helmet as well.

"The air's a little stale," he said, taking a deep breath.

They undressed, removing their suits, which returned to a soft silk texture. They both folded their spacesuits in a neat pile, and she took a step toward the table.

"Wait," Brian said, and then embraced her in a hug before letting her go. "I'm so happy you're here. I've been missing you for months and this seems like a dream come true."

"Missed you too," Cora said, as her face grew hot. "I'm happy to finally have some time with you without our chaperones."

He chuckled.

"Aunt Ferna and my dad mean well," he said, strolling to the table.

They made it to the table and grabbed a seat each. Cora scrolled through the menu of the meal crafter.

"Coffee and cookies?" she asked in an ironic tone. "I wonder who filled this meal crafter?"

"I thought it best to put our favorite foods in here," he said with a lopsided smile. "By the way, you have coffee and I have six types of fruit cookies: apricot, raspberry, lemon, strawberry—"

"Okay, I believe you." Cora giggled and selected coffee from the menu. "Oh, you have a plain cookie."

"Of course, I know you don't like desserts that are too sweet," he snickered. "I still think that doesn't make any sense, but..." His voice trailed off as he selected coffee and a raspberry butter cookie.

"Hmm..." she said, biting into a soft, buttery cookie.

"I know," Brian said. I found a new recipe for that perfect balance of buttery and crumbly.

"When it comes to moving to Mars, are there other things you're thinking about?" she asked, sinking her teeth into a second cookie.

"Well, sort of," he said, swallowing the last of his coffee. "Apart from you and dad, I'm also thinking about the Albright Corporation. Dad still thinks it's going to implode. He thinks Jessica Spencer's immoral behavior will destroy it."

Jessica ran Spencer Industries and had a huge influence on Albright Corporation. Brian had worked with Jessica for several months, trying to persuade her not to do something illegal, but in the end, he had failed. As a result, his mom had fired him from his family's business.

"I don't know if that's true," Cora said. "Entire governments exist for hundreds of years with no sense of morality."

"I agree with you and Dad, but not equally," Brian said, pursing his lips in thought. "There's something about Dad's words that still bothers me. I really think he's right, and there's something kind of unhinged about Jessica. The real problem is there's nobody to check her. Nobody stands up to her. I know it makes little sense."

"I see," she said. "That's a good point about Jessica. The few times I've dealt with her, she's been angry—I mean like something boiling beneath the surface type of fury. I don't think she's crazy, though. Instead, I think she's deeply unhappy."

"I also have concerns about my sister, Eliza," he said. "She's taken over Albright Corporation and Mining. I don't think she truly understood how involved the corporate side could be. It involves managing spoiled Askovs and Askovians with abilities that could hurt her."

"So, you want to hang around in case they need your help?" she asked.

"Maybe..." he sighed. "I don't know. I have all these thoughts whirling around in my head. On the one hand, I think it would be better if I followed my dad and ran away. Let both the Corporation and mining operations collapse on themselves. But somehow I just can't do it. I don't know why."

"I have a theory or hypothesis maybe...," she said and paused, gathering her thoughts. "Sometimes Aunt Ferna has ideas not based on what everyone knows. She gets a hunch and that hunch nine times out of ten turns out to be true. I think that hunch is her latent Feeler abilities. I wonder if you have a little of your mom's Feeler abilities. Maybe yours aren't as pronounced, but they are there all the same."

"I don't know about that," he said with a chuckle.

"Don't you find your hunches are generally true?" Cora asked.

"Well... When I have a strong hunch about something, it's true," Brian said. "Doesn't that make me a Seer?

Cora wrinkled her nose while Brian guffawed. Askovs debated Seer's abilities. Some felt they could see into the past and future, while others felt they were charlatans. Cora didn't trust them at all.

"You know, based on how I'm feeling, the best thing may be that both businesses fail," he said with a shrug.

"Maybe you're right about Albright," she said. "But that doesn't also mean you should abandon your mom and sister."

"But this is becoming—" he said and paused when they heard distorted music echoing inside their tent.

"What was that?" she asked.

"It's the doorbell for our tent. It's meant to be a song, but something's broken," he said, reaching for his comm bracelet and launching the vidchat.

"This is Brian Farris. May I ask who you are?" he asked.

A moment later, three clear bubbles each filled with a face crammed together to fit onto Brian's screen.

"Hello, we're Tom and Maria Stanley," he said. He was a thirty-something man with a thin face and a receding jet-black hairline. "We wondered if we could come inside for a moment." Tom said, glancing at the little girl. "Vie is tired and needs a little break."

Maria looked about Tom's age, with a full face and curly, light-brown hair. Their daughter, Vie, was a cute seven-year-old with curly jet-black hair.

Cora raised both eyebrows, but Brian waved a hand at her.

"Is something wrong?" he asked. "Does Vie need medical help?"

"No, nothing like that," Tom said, chuckling.

"Of course," Brian said. "Do you know how to unlatch the outer door?"

"Yes, thank you very much," Tom said.

Cora listened to the whooshing sound of air from the outer door opening and closing.

"It's considered common courtesy to host travelers when you have a tent," Brian said. "Sometimes it's because of an injury, so I had to make sure."

"I guess, but it seems odd to allow a stranger into your tent," Cora said as air brushed past her from the opening inner door.

Three bubble-headed humans walked into their tent. Cora and Brian stood to greet them.

"How do you do?" Brian asked. "This is Cora." He gestured to her.

All three of them removed their helmets, but Cora couldn't sense their emotions at all. They must be Originals, but why would they install a neurowall in a child?

"Please come in and have a seat," Cora said.

"We camped overnight and had a long hike down the side of the mountain," Tom said with a small smile. "Vie's become more and more irritable throughout the morning, and we thought if she could get out of her spacesuit for a few minutes she'd be okay."

"I'm Tom's wife, Maria," the brown-haired woman said, taking a couple of steps toward the table when Tom's hand shot out and rested on her shoulder.

"Just a minute, are you Coraline Brimble?" Tom asked.

Maria turned to face Cora and her face blanched.

"Oh, I didn't recognize you," Maria said and turned to her husband. "Tom?"

"We're sorry to bother you. We'll be leaving now," Tom said.

What's wrong with everyone here? she thought as she surveyed Tom and Maria scrambling to put their helmets on and force one on Vie. Tom then struggled to carry his daughter through the door.

"No! I'm tired. I want to stay," Vie whimpered.

"Sorry, honey," Tom said. "I'll carry you the rest of the way." He turned to the inner door of the tent while his wife fumbled with the latch. The latches finally separated, and the three of them stumbled into the chamber. They stayed there for a few minutes because Maria hadn't re-engaged all the latches on the inner door, which meant the outer door wouldn't open. Visibly frustrated, Tom re-latched the inner door for her and the three of them fled the chamber. Cora watched as Tom re-latched the outer chamber.

"Aunt wasn't kidding," she said. "Tensions are high here. It's so ridiculous. We can't even enjoy casual friendships."

"I'm sorry about that," Brian said with a sigh. "I didn't realize they'd react that way."

"You have nothing to apologize for," Cora said. "But I have a terrible feeling about the state of things between the Originals and Askovs."

CHAPTER 5

Two days later, Cora sat on the gray and white sofa in the suite's living room, wearing a soft powder-blue short-sleeved shirt with matching pants. She leaned back on the sofa with her feet on the coffee table surrounded by three floating screens. After breakfast, Brian had rushed off to meet a client, Benjamin to join his friend Omar, and Aunt Ferna to visit Kenna and catch up on gossip.

On one floating screen, Cora checked her game, Mystery Adventures, verifying that the game's AI resolved all player issues. She used the second screen to review a monthly report from Brimble Mining. Noticing a worrying trend in the decreasing alythium, she evaluated the report a second time.

The third screen displayed the results of a search through the Net for Aria Spencer. Cora focused on this screen, combing through her entire background. Aria was an Askovian whose DNA had been adjusted for the conventionally beautiful look most Askovs desired. She had flawless skin, symmetrical facial features, and straight brown hair. Aria had also run a consulting business where she helped other Askovs learn to create what she called star music. Listening to some of it, Cora thought it sounded very generic and bland.

I suppose the process of creating the music was complex, she thought. *My guess is that's what her clients paid her for.*

Suddenly, the door to the suite slid open with a whoosh of air, causing her to sit up straight and remove her feet from the coffee table. Now, she could see over the top of all the screens, and she watched as Steven Marsh entered the suite. He was a pale faced, thin, thirty-something man with dull brown hair.

"I thought I'd seen you in the spaceport," Cora said with furrowed eyebrows. "Aren't you taking risks showing yourself in public like this?"

"Technically, I'm not in public," Steven said with a genial smile. "To answer your question, this is Lunar City, and the EGS has no jurisdiction here."

"The EGS and the IPS tend to work together," she said. "Why wouldn't the IPS turn you in?"

He grinned and plopped onto one of the overstuffed chairs facing Cora. She closed all the floating screens.

"Because, my dear, the IPS needs me," he said, surveying the meal crafter in the center of the coffee table. "Do you have any coffee?"

Cora gestured to the meal crafter. Steven leaned over the table, selected a button, and collected his cup.

"So, I notice I can't read your emotions at all," she said. "You must have a very high-grade neurowall."

"The best I could steal from the military," he said, chuckling. "By the way, good coffee."

"Out of curiosity, is that the same level of neurowall protection the Originals are using?" she asked.

"No, not all Originals," he said, taking a sip. "But the ones with piles of credits definitely purchase the higher-grade black-market version. I may've profited from a few of those transactions." He grinned. "The IPS provides a cheaper low-quality version, but at least two Readers have invaded the minds of Originals using that version."

"So, what exactly are you doing here?" Cora asked.

"Oh yes," he said, turning away from her for a moment. "This has to do with Aria Spencer. I decided to take a look into her death. There's something not right."

"I agree," Cora said. "It's highly suspicious, but why'd you care?"

"I'm afraid I might be responsible for what actually killed her," Steven said, pursing his lips. "I want to make sure that I'm safe from any IPS retaliation. Would you look into her death?"

"Jane Spencer was here a few days ago asking me to do the same thing," she sighed. "But I turned her down and I'm telling you the same thing. I'm here for a pleasant vacation, and I don't want to expose myself to another killer."

"I understand that," he said, raising both hands to stop her. "But this is very serious. I doubt Aria will be the last person murdered. If I'm correct and this has something to do with me, then her murder will be the beginning of a string of strange deaths."

"What have you done?" she asked with an edge to her voice. Cora chided herself for asking as it awakened that familiar tingle of excitement at deciphering a new puzzle or fresh investigation.

Steven stood and paced around the living room before stepping to the back of his chair. He stood behind it, gripping the upholstery tightly.

"I helped someone smuggle a lot of military tech into Lunar City," he sighed. "It's the reason so many Originals have high-grade neurowalls. But I didn't pay attention to the entire load when it arrived several months ago. A few packages went missing and I don't know what they contained. Given that it was military tech, it could've been something that'd make a person drop dead."

"Who helped you?" she asked, feeling herself giving into the pull to untangle this mystery.

"I don't know," he scowled. "All transactions were anonymous, which seemed like a good idea before. Then I noticed the discrepancies, and... Well, somehow I lost control."

"The more you talk, the less I want to help," she frowned. "This sounds like a lunatic on the loose with advanced tech ready to murder. Someone I'll never see coming. Why not get the IPS involved, since they seem to love you?"

"They love me as long as they believe I'm not breaking any laws," he scowled. "They keep multiple monitors on me, and I have to work to evade them. I can't afford to have them disillusioned. I'd have two government agencies against me."

Cora chuckled at his words. "Disillusioned?" she asked.

"I can't tell you everything, but it's very serious," Steven said. "I also don't want to put you in danger, and I don't want you to go snooping. Instead, I'd just like you to have conversations with Aria's friends and family. Right now, I'm interested in one friend, Porter. He owns a tech company and is the only one of her friends with enough hacker experience to pull off the theft. He's an Askov, but he's friendly with Originals. Funneling a lot of tech to Originals, there's a chance he's dangerous. I don't want you involved. I only want you to notice anything unusual that he may be saying."

"How do you know he's funneling neurowalls to the Originals?" Cora asked, folding her arms, while waging another battle with herself. One side of her wanted to jump in and help. The other wanted to live a quiet life.

"Not everything I do is legal," he said with a small smile. "If things go wrong, the less you know the better."

"I'm not saying I'll help, but who's Porter's family?" she asked, lowering her arms.

"Upton," he said. "They're Listeners, but he has no abilities. Do you know them?"

"Yes, I know of them," she said as a tiny spark at the idea nudged her to find the killer. "I've met his mom and dad a few times at meetings."

"Sometime in the next few days, Jane is going to ask you again to help her," he said. "Please say yes. Tell her you'll talk to a few of her friends and family. But let me know what you're doing. I don't want you in any danger."

Cora nodded, accepting she'd lost the war with herself.

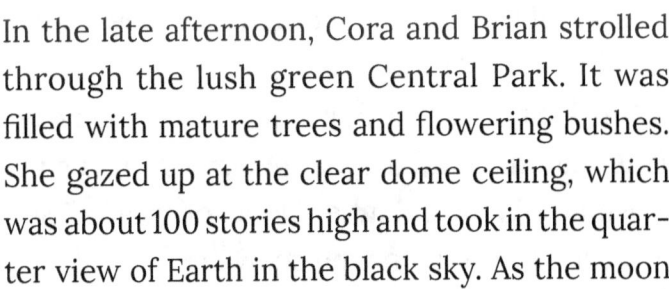

In the late afternoon, Cora and Brian strolled through the lush green Central Park. It was filled with mature trees and flowering bushes. She gazed up at the clear dome ceiling, which was about 100 stories high and took in the quarter view of Earth in the black sky. As the moon continued its orbit, that visible sliver of Earth would get smaller with the passing days.

"I think this is my favorite part of Lunar City," Cora said with a happy sigh as a lightness spread throughout her chest. Grinning, she squeezed Brian's hand, listening to the creek trickling near their path.

"Well, wait until you've seen the rest of it." Brian chuckled.

"How much time do we have before we meet Aunt Ferna and your dad?" she asked, stepping along the path toward a tiny pond.

"Less than an hour now," he said. "But the restaurant's a bit of a walk from here."

"Okay—is that Jane coming toward us?" she asked, turning toward a woman approaching them.

"I think you're right," he smirked. "She looks so much like Jessica, but I won't hold it against her."

"It's as if the Spencer women are clones," Cora said in a joking tone of voice.

"Cora. Brian. I'm so surprised to see you here," Jane said in a mild drawl. She gave them a sunny smile. "You remember Drew, of course." She gestured to the man who scowled.

Cora didn't believe for one minute their meeting was an accident. But she also couldn't figure out how Jane tracked her down.

"I don't think this is a good idea, Jane," Drew said with the same lunar accent. "Let's get out of here."

"Nonsense," Jane said and turned to Cora. "So, have you thought about what I asked? Will you help? Please say yes!"

Jane reached out and grabbed one of Cora's hands. Cora, having gone to school with several Readers, understood what she was trying to do. Many Readers detected thoughts with ease when they were in physical contact with their target. However, Cora had also learned how to block them.

"Cora, think about it," Jane frowned. She'd tried to detect Cora's thoughts but poorly masked her disappointment at being blocked. She quickly recovered and continued. "Aria was only two years older than me and in perfect health. Then suddenly, with nobody around her, she just drops dead. What happened to her?" She scowled.

"What does the IPS think happened to her?" Cora asked.

"Their initial analysis at the scene didn't reveal any poisons or harm to her body," Jane said. "Since Aria had no nanobots to protect her, they think a Reader manipulated her brain into causing her heart to stop." She frowned. "At least that's what Agent Taylor thinks. Although that's possible, a Reader that powerful would have to be in physical contact with her in order to do that. But she was alone."

Nanobots were tiny robots less than a millimeter high programmed to perform specialized tasks. These activities included maintaining regular functioning of internal organs or performing necessary repairs to save a life.

"If you don't think it was a Reader," Cora said. "What do you think happened?"

"I don't know," Jane sighed. "I've been racking my brain for days now and can't figure out what happened."

"Also, it's not true that a Reader would have to be in physical contact with her," Brian said. "I've met plenty of powerful Readers that could have put that suggestion in her head at a distance."

"True. But wouldn't we have heard of a Reader like that?" Cora asked.

"I've heard rumors of Readers like that in the Casino Dome," Jane said, staring at the neighboring creek. "But they work for large amounts of credits."

Drew scoffed.

"Well, do you have a better idea?" Jane asked, her lips set in a straight line. "You think she dropped dead for no reason?"

"No, I didn't say that," Drew crossed his arms. "I think Aria's life should remain private."

"Oh, is that what you're afraid of?" Jane asked, glaring at Drew. "Finding out who murdered my sister is more important than your embarrassment." She turned to Cora. "What do you think?"

"I have a couple of ideas," Cora said. "But what's this about embarrassment?"

"What? I thought we agreed you wouldn't get involved with this case," Brian said, exasperation in his voice.

"Yes, but something came up," Cora said and turned back to Jane. "I've thought about it and decided to help you."

Brian grumbled under his breath.

"Oh, thank you. Thank you so much!" Jane bounced on her heels and grabbed Cora's hand again. "I really appreciate it. Somebody is behind this, and I only want justice for my sister. Please let me know anything that you might need."

"I understand a private funeral will take place in the next few days," Cora said. "Can you get a list of who will be at that funeral? Then we might cross reference with the people at the spaceport when Aria passed. My thought is if a Reader killed her, maybe they need to be close to their victim."

"You're saying someone in the Spencer family killed her?" Drew asked. "That's silly."

"I'm saying most murders are committed by someone the victim knows," Cora said. "Funerals usually include immediate family and very close friends." She paused, meeting his eyes. "So, want to tell me what you're embarrassed about?"

Drew scowled at her.

"Well, I think it's a great idea," Jane said, glaring at Drew. She turned to Cora. "Maybe I can even get that stupid Agent Taylor to help us." She sighed. "I wish she wasn't so focused on me. There are Readers all over Lunar City, and they're not all related to me." She glanced behind Cora.

"Porter. What are you doing here?" Jane said to two men approaching.

Jane hugged the first man, who wore a confused expression. He was in his mid-twenties, an average height, with flawless bronze skin, shiny curly black hair, and symmetrical brown eyes. His confusion further confirmed Cora's suspicion that Jane must have arranged for everyone to meet here.

"Cora. Brian. This is Porter," Jane said with a friendly smile. "I don't normally see him out of his computer lab." The three nodded to each other.

"I'm so sorry for your loss," Porter said.

"So, what are you doing here, Porter?" Drew asked with a condescending smile.

"How are you doing?" Porter asked with a forced smile. "It's been a while since we've met."

"Yeah, that's because you've been avoiding me," Drew said with an edge to his voice.

"I haven't been avoiding you," Porter rubbed his face with both hands. He looked as if he hadn't slept well. "I've been working. We recently released a new version of our software. Gavin came back from Earth a few days ago with another round of funding."

"When do you think you'll be able to pay me?" Drew scowled.

"Do you really want to have this conversation here?" Jane replied instead of Porter. "Cora. Brian. This is Linus."

A handsome, tall, muscular man in his mid-twenties with auburn hair stepped forward and hugged Jane. She made a brief hug and stepped away from him.

"So sorry for your loss," Linus mumbled while staring at the ground.

"Why did you start carrying a blaster again?" Jane asked.

Linus shrugged. On his hip hung a small black and silver blaster, which was unusual for Askovs.

"I don't appreciate you interrupting me," Drew said to Jane and then turned to Porter. "What you don't understand is I need those credits. I've been listening to your excuses for months now."

"You're right. I owe you credits, and I'm long overdue paying you back," Porter said with a placating voice. "I don't have them right now. But our investors have confirmed our next round of funding, and I'll have the credits for you in the next few weeks."

"So, what's everybody doing here today?" Linus asked in a lunar drawl, his eyes shifting from Drew to Porter.

Linus was trying to change the subject, but it's clear Jane didn't tell him about the meeting in the park, Cora thought. *I wonder why.*

"I happened to run into Cora and Brian," Jane said in a chipper voice. "She's going to look into Aria's death. I know something happened to her."

Cora couldn't lower her shield to sense Jane's lie, but she was sure of it.

"Do you work for the IPS?" Porter asked.

"Hardly," Drew sneered. "She's just one of Jane's little friends who happened to figure out a couple of murders last year."

"Wow! That's impressive," Porter said with a charming smile. "I've never solved an actual crime before. I hope you do find out what happened to Aria. But I also hope it was only an accident."

"Is that why you're here?" Linus asked with a furtive glance toward Cora.

"I'm actually on vacation from Earth," Cora said, wondering at his shyness. "I thought the council banned blasters in Lunar City to protect the domes."

"They're allowed with special permission," Linus said, shifting from foot-to-foot as more eyes turned his way.

"What you don't understand is Cora is famous," Jane said, turning the conversation away from Linus. "She single-handedly figured out who killed four people. This was despite all the efforts from the EGS."

"Of course, I've heard of you." Porter chuckled. "I didn't know you were a detective, but I've played Mystery Adventures. I've spent hours trying to figure out your puzzles. It's a good game."

Cora turned a little pink with his compliments.

"Porter. I thought you'd already be at the cafe," an average-looking man said, approaching from the direction the other two had come. He was in his late thirties with a round face, receding brown hairline and hazel eyes.

"Gavin. Come here and meet some new friends," Porter said. "This is Coraline Brimble."

"Oh yes. You wrote Mystery Adventures," Gavin said with a cheerful smile. "I spend way too many hours avoiding work with that game."

"I'll take that as a compliment," Cora said with a chortle.

"We're on our way to the Lunar Bakery," Porter said. "Want to join us?"

"We can't. We're meeting someone for dinner," Brian said. "Actually, if we don't leave now, we'll be late."

"Come on. The guys are waiting," Gavin said, stepping away from their impromptu group.

"It was good seeing you all," Porter said. He turned and jogged to catch up with Gavin.

As they left the conversation, Cora compared the men. Gavin looked like a normal human, an Original. Whereas Drew, Porter, and Linus' parents had clearly modified them to fit into society's attractive standards.

"What are you still doing here?" Jane said in a curt voice to Linus, who shrugged a shoulder.

Why does he need a blaster and why doesn't Jane like him? Cora thought.

"I'll catch up with you later," Linus said as he turned and trudged off the way he'd come.

"I'm sorry for the interruption," Jane said, turning to Cora. "I'll get what you asked for and send it to you as soon as possible." She turned to Drew. "Let's go."

Jane and Drew strolled down a different path and soon disappeared among the foliage.

"There's a story with these friends," Cora said, tilting her head. "I'm going to discover it."

CHAPTER 6

The following morning, Cora stepped out of her bedroom, wearing a midnight blue top and white pants. She paused when she saw Brian sitting alone at the dining room table. He looked up and gave her a small smile. A heaviness settled on her chest as she sensed his grumpy mood.

"Morning," Cora said, walking around the sofa and grabbing the chair across from him. "Did you sleep well?" She glanced at the empty table, wondering why he wasn't eating breakfast.

"Okay," Brian said with a frown. "Look, Cora, I want to talk about yesterday. Why did you agree to help Jane?"

Yesterday, after they'd left the park, Aunt Ferna had met them on their way and joined them for the walk to the restaurant. Cora hadn't felt comfortable explaining to Brian why she'd changed her mind. Aunt Ferna would worry about her involvement in another murder, and Aunt Ferna didn't like Steven.

"Yeah, I'm sorry this went on so long," she said, leaning her elbows onto the table. "Yesterday, Stephen Marsh visited me."

"Steven!" he said with raised eyebrows. "Is he back?"

"I'm afraid so," she said with a half-smile. "It seems trouble always follows Steven."

"Maybe he shouldn't break the law," he said sarcastically.

"That would fix most of his problems," she said, removing her elbows and sitting upright. "Actually, that's the real reason he showed up. He was involved with doing something... illegal. Things didn't go as planned, and a bunch of stolen tech disappeared. He's afraid he might be responsible for Aria's death. He told me, he worked with a partner, but they never knew each other's identity. Instead, they used aliases. So, he doesn't exactly know what's missing, but he knows it's some sort of military tech."

"Figures," Brian said, leaning back in his chair with a huff. "I'm so tired of that guy. In the end, this is Steven's problem. Why should you help him?"

"I don't know," Cora said, glancing at the ceiling. "Call it a hunch. I have a bad feeling that if I do nothing, a lot more people are going to die. He kept emphasizing how deadly the military tech could be."

"I still don't like this," he said. "This is a case where there's some technology owned by a lunatic who's planning to kill people and you're proposing to put yourself in harm's way."

"Not exactly," she said. "The plan is for me to only talk to her friends and any family members who may be involved. If I discover anything odd, I'll report it to him, and he can handle it from there."

"You've chased two criminals now," he said, peeved. "How many of them put your life in danger?"

"Both," she said with a sigh.

"Exactly," he scowled. "This won't end well even if you try to stay safe."

"I agree with you," she said in a quiet voice. "But I've learned a lot from my last two encounters, and I'll take more precautions. I also don't plan to create and follow an investigation. I'm only going to have conversations."

A moment of silence elapsed between them.

"Okay, here's an idea," Brian said, reaching across the table. His hand held hers for a moment before he continued. "Let's work together, have these conversations, and talk to Steven. I want to make sure you're not alone with any of Aria's friends or family."

"That's a great idea," Cora said with a bright smile as a weight lifted from her chest. "We can spend more time together, and I'd feel a lot safer."

"Hello, you two," Aunt Ferna said as she bustled into the room. "How did you both sleep?"

"Good," Cora said, releasing Brian's hand.

He mumbled something under his breath while Cora sensed his mild irritation.

"Today, you and I are going to meet Kenna," Aunt Ferna said, plopping onto a seat between Cora and Brian.

"Oh?" Cora asked. "I might've met her before in Tymal. She's from the Yarmouth family?"

"Yes, she's Drew's aunt on his dad's side," Aunt Ferna said. "I've known the family for years. We were in school together."

"I look forward to meeting her," Cora said. "Is she a Mover like the rest of the Yarmouths?"

"Yes, dear," Aunt Ferna said. "But she's not as powerful as her nephew. In any case, the reason

I want you to accompany me is that she knows what's going on before anyone else. She's also been influential in many business and marriage deals. As head of Brimble Mining, it'd help to get to know her." She turned to Brian. "You might get more clients, too, if you wanted to come along."

Aunt Ferna selected a cup of tea and a blueberry scone from the meal crafter.

Neither Cora nor Brian had selected their breakfasts yet. Cora selected a cup of coffee, scrambled eggs, and toast. Lunar City eggs had a hint of something, giving them a different flavor profile, and she still wasn't used to them.

Brian selected a plain scone and a cup of coffee from the crafter.

As they ate, Cora sensed Brian's mood lighten with the food. He gave her a sheepish grin when they exchanged glances.

"When do you want to leave, aunt?" Cora asked.

"Another hour or so will be fine," Aunt Ferna said, finishing the last of her scone.

"I wish I could go with you two," Brian said with a frown. "But I've got a meeting with a client in a couple of hours, and I need time to prepare." He turned to Cora. "I know you'll be safe with Aunt Ferna. But let me know if you run into Drew. I really don't like that guy."

"You want a play-by-play report?" she asked with a lopsided smile.

"No, I want you to be safe," he stood and kissed her on the forehead and stepped into his bedroom.

"What was that about?" Aunt Ferna asked in a hushed voice.

Before Cora could answer, he emerged from his bedroom with a small bag slung over one shoulder.

"Have a good time," he said, stepping out the suite's door.

"What was that about being safe?" Aunt Ferna asked again.

Cora hesitated to tell her aunt—she didn't want her to worry.

"A few days ago, Jane Spencer asked me to help look into what happened to Aria," Cora said, holding up both arms as her aunt's face became etched with worry. "It's alright. I promise I won't do anything dangerous." She sighed. "Brian's upset because I agreed to help Jane. When she asked the first time, I told her no, but later I agreed."

"In this case, I agree with Brian," Aunt Ferna said, her eyebrows furrowed. "I know you always do what you want to do, but I saw exactly how that poor girl died. I think it was a Reader, a powerful Reader. You can't protect yourself against that."

Cora reached across the table just as Brian had earlier and squeezed her aunt's hand. She waited until she sensed her aunt calming.

"Sorry to worry you," Cora said in a gentle voice. "I don't want to end up in danger again. My intention is to hold conversations with certain friends and family."

Fortunately, Aunt Ferna didn't ask any more questions, and Cora avoided mentioning Steven Marsh's involvement.

An hour later, Aunt Ferna and Cora strolled from the walkway that separated Lunar City's Central Park from Athos Tower. They turned down a small path into the gray, uniform Askov neighborhood.

"I don't think I could live here," Cora said, wrinkling her nose. "There's only a sea of gray rectangular boxes they call homes, and no greenery anywhere."

"That's because you're looking at the outside." Aunt Ferna chuckled. "The inside will remind you of home. Askovs take a lot of trouble to import vegetation from Earth. It'll look like a little park when we step inside. You'll see what I mean."

These neighborhoods differed from what Cora was used to. In Tymal, the Askov neighborhoods featured large homes on large lots surrounded by mature trees and flowering bushes. Instead, these Lunar City neighborhoods featured lots of tall narrow homes that almost filled their lots and varied only in height and shades of gray.

As they reached the Yarmouth home, the home's AI activated.

"Aunt Ferna and Coraline Brimble," the home's AI said in a deep male voice. "You are expected. Please enter." The front door slid open.

They stepped inside and Cora chortled at the forest-like entryway. She spun in a slow circle, taking in the ferns, vines, and lilies. Inhaling the cool, moist air, she turned to Aunt Ferna with a broad smile.

"Ferna, my dear, it's so good to see you," Kenna said, surrounding Aunt Ferna with a gentle embrace. Kenna was around the same age as Aunt Ferna. They looked similar with their short stature and rounded hips, but they differed in other ways. Kenna's light-blue eyes and pale skin contrasted with Aunt Ferna's brown eyes and bronze skin.

"This is my niece, Cora," Aunt Ferna said, gesturing to her. "I think she's in love with your foyer."

All three women giggled.

"It reminds me of home," Cora said, rubbing one arm. "It even feels good on my skin."

"Yes, we have humidity control throughout our home," Kenna said, turning from Cora to Aunt Ferna. "The air can get so dry here in Lunar city."

"I think you two have met before," Aunt Ferna said.

"Yes, briefly," Kenna replied. "In Tymal, we attended some boring meeting run by Jessica. I couldn't wait till it ended, so I could go shopping."

Kenna linked arms with Aunt Ferna and they walked side-by-side down a short hall. Cora followed and marveled at the dark red carpet, brown faux wood-paneled walls, and images of ancient ancestors trimmed in gold. She expected this style on Earth, but not on the moon, in a space colony.

This must've cost a fortune to bring up here, she thought.

Cora followed them into a small sitting room that looked like something from her own home. It featured two large sofas facing each other and covered in floral print, a large ornate faux wood coffee table, and two additional overstuffed chairs paired together around a tiny round table. The wall, covered with a pale-yellow wallpaper, featured tiny white flowers.

Cora lowered her shield and swept the house with her abilities. Only the three women were in the house.

"My dear, are you hungry?" Kenna asked, sitting next to Aunt Ferna.

"I could do with a cup of tea," Aunt Ferna said, settling herself onto one sofa.

"Maybe a cup of coffee," Cora said, lowering onto the opposite sofa. "I've just had breakfast."

Kenna operated the meal crafter, which produced a cup of coffee, two cups of tea, and a plate of cinnamon rolls.

"Based on the last mining report, Bimble Mining appears to remain healthy and profitable," Kenna said with a small smile. "You must have good management at the site."

"Yes, I got lucky with them," Cora said. "They're good at anticipating problems and letting me know how they have or will address them."

"Excellent. I think we've all benefited from Albright's management," Kenna said, alluding to Harold and Brian's previous management. Harold Albright used to run the Albright Corporation, which provided mining management to several small mines, including Cora's. "Now, my dear, I heard Jane has asked you to look into her sister's death."

Even though she had accepted her comings and goings would become gossip, Cora didn't expect news to travel that fast.

"Don't you think that's dangerous?" Kenna asked, taking a sip of tea.

"It's definitely dangerous," Cora said, sensing a mild malicious intent in Kenna's words. "But I don't intend to do a full investigation, so I'm hoping I'll stay safe. I also plan to turn in all of my findings to the IPS."

This wasn't exactly true, but Cora felt as if she was speaking to the rest of Lunar City and needed to make sure everything appeared as if she followed the law.

"Well, I'm happy to hear that," Kenna said and turned to Aunt Ferna, cutting Cora out of the rest of the conversation. "Have you heard the latest?"

Aunt Ferna shook her head.

"You remember me mentioning Trudy?" Kenna asked, becoming animated at the new topic. "It turns out a few days ago she left for Earth. Can you believe it?"

"Who's Trudy?" Cora asked, sensing an increase in Kenna's malevolence.

"Well..." Kenna paused for a moment, as if to gather her thoughts. "It seems my innocent nephew... You know Drew?"

Cora nodded.

"Well, he became entangled with one of those Originals," Kenna wrinkled her nose. "Trudy seduced him for months. When Aria found out, she threatened to break things off with him. It was a mess."

This is all Trudy's fault? Cora thought with a frown.

"I understand. The Spencer family wanted to end their engagement," Aunt Ferna said.

"Of course, and who could blame them?" Kenna asked. "But my brother forced Drew to apologize to the entire family while publicly humiliating Trudy. They also had to agree to a lower marriage settlement. The controversy continued for three months, only ending when Trudy left."

"I understand the Originals are a little conservative," Aunt Ferna said. "Her family must've subjected her to fairly bad treatment."

"Well, I don't care," Kenna said, munching on a cinnamon roll. "I'm just glad she's gone. She could have ended a very lucrative alliance between two families, all for some fun. I spoke to Drew and made it clear he'd risked his entire future for an Original. He should've known better."

Cora gazed at Kenna, nonplussed. Askov families sometimes arranged marriages, and it usually involved a financial transaction. But she'd never been involved in discussions. She forced herself not to reply to Kenna's cold view of the relationship between Drew and Aria, and the suffering Trudy must've endured.

She also wasn't prepared for the amount of vitriol about Originals from Kenna. She wondered why Aunt Ferna stayed friends with her. Then a thought crossed her mind.

"Kenna, I'm a little confused about something," Cora said. "Why were Drew and Aria at the spaceport?"

"They had plans for a mini vacation," Kenna said. "They were supposed to restart their relationship to get over the damage done by that Trudy. Also Aria asked for time to think about continuing with the engagement." She took another bite of her roll. "I know from Drew's point of view he still wanted to marry, but I'm less sure about Aria."

"If I'm not being too intrusive," Cora asked. "Would it have been a hardship for Drew to receive fewer credits from the marriage?"

"No, more of an inconvenience," Kenna said. "There's income from our mines to support our entire family. But additional credits properly invested would've helped with future children or starting any other future business endeavors."

"I wondered if the Yarmouth or Spencer families would've benefited from Aria's death," Cora said with a thoughtful expression.

"What?" Kenna asked in a raised voice with pinched lips. "Are you implying that one of us would try to kill Aria?"

"I'm not trying to imply anything," Cora said, keeping her own tone level. "Someone killed Aria, and statistically, the victim usually knows the murderer. The most logical place to look is her friends and family."

Kenna glared at Cora, her mouth set in a straight line.

"She didn't really mean anything," Aunt Ferna said, patting Kenna's hand.

Cora stifled a sigh. She'd expected Aunt Ferna to take her friend's side. Although Aunt Ferna loved her, she sometimes put her friends first.

"Let me give you an example," Cora said. "What if Jessica Spencer would've benefited because Aria owned a certain percentage of the family mine?" She chose the least likely suspect so as not to upset Kenna again.

"I see," Kenna said, slightly mollified. "I know there's no benefit to anybody inside Aria's immediate family. We reviewed their finances when discussing marriage terms. Aria's dad and Jessica had a huge falling out even before Aria and Jane were born. They agreed to sever joint finances permanently."

"Also, the Yarmouths won't receive any credits now the marriage won't take place," Cora said, gauging Kenna's emotions. She noted a spike in Kenna's anger that she tried to cover up with a forced smile.

"I wondered how you did your investigations," Kenna said. "It's thrilling to see that I was part of the inquiries. I'll have to let my friends know."

She turned to Aunt Ferna, and they launched into another round of gossip.

The rest of their get-together went as expected with Aunt Ferna and Kenna, chit-chatting while Cora let her mind wander to the Spencer family and Aria's parents.

CHAPTER 7

A couple of days later, Cora stepped through the front doors of the Lunar Herbivore, a restaurant that only served vegetables grown in the lunar soil. Even the coffee beans grew in lunar soil. This supposedly gave the food and drinks a certain quality that only those with discriminating palates could taste, according to Aunt Ferna.

She scanned the small restaurant before spotting Jane and strolled toward her. Cora passed tables set amongst trees and vines that were part of the Lunar Herbivore's decor.

"Cora. I'm so happy to see you here," Jane said. She stood to greet her with a hug.

"It's good to see you too," Cora said. "How are funeral arrangements coming along?"

"Oh, you know," Jane said as her smile faltered. "Mom is upset. Dad is not being helpful.

But we have other family members who've been planning things."

"I'm very sorry," Cora said with a frown. "I lost a sister too." What Cora didn't mention was she wasn't too sad about it. Her sister had been a horrible, mean bully. But Cora left all that off.

"So, have you been here before?" Jane asked.

"No, no, I haven't," Cora said. "Brian's been taking me to a new place every day, but we haven't made it here."

"They've the best crystallized vegetables," Jane said. "I love the way they crunch. I always go for their vegetable medley. It's sort of like a cooked salad mixed with little bits of bread. All of it's grown here."

"Where're they growing all these vegetables?" Cora asked.

"It's so fascinating," Jane said with enthusiasm. "Growers have specialized domes spread all over the moon, whose only function is food production. They're run by AIs who monitor and control local gravity, moisture, lighting, and nutritional levels each plant needs—like specialized greenhouses."

Cora recalled seeing specialized greenhouses on Earth, but imagined these would need more provisions to defend the plants against the moon's nonexistent atmosphere.

"Now, some growers specialize in soil," Jane said, leaning in as she warmed to the subject. "This restaurant uses a grower who concentrates on lunar soil."

"So, the plants grow in primarily lunar soil, but with added nutrients?" Cora asked.

"Of course not. These plants are all adapted to Earth's environment," Jane said in a condescending tone, giving Cora flashbacks of every conversation she'd had with Jessica Spencer. "Farmers grow the plants in Earth soil with added nutrients and added lunar soil."

"I see," Cora said. "Well, according to my aunt, she can taste the difference when the plants grow in lunar or Martian soil."

Light peals of laughter escape Jane's lips.

"My mom says the same thing," Jane said. "I think it's just that generation. They're trying to prove they're somehow special. I haven't figured it out." Jane pressed a button on the meal crafter. "Anyway, do you need time to look at the menu?"

"I looked at it before I got here," Cora said. "I'm going to get the crystallized salad."

"That's my favorite," Jane said. "I'm getting the same thing."

They both took their turn at the crafter. Cora selected the crystallized vegetable medley with mango juice. Jane chose the same thing except with water. As they were eating, Drew sauntered into the restaurant and took a seat at their table.

"I thought you'd take her here," Drew said. "I thought I told you I didn't want you to talk to her."

"You're clearly confused," Jane said in a scolding voice. "You think you're my father. And even my father wouldn't dare tell me who I can talk to. Since you're here, you can either keep your mouth shut or you can leave." Jane spoke with a complete air of authority that would have made Jessica Spencer proud.

Drew shifted in his chair, reached for the crafter, and scrolled for food options. He mumbled something under his breath that sounded like a muffled apology. Cora finished her meal.

"Would you mind if I asked you some questions?" Cora asked.

Jane finished her plate and put it in the recycling. She took a sip of water and nodded.

"Did you notice anything strange on the day that your sister passed?" Cora said in a very gentle voice.

Jane paused, looking down at her glass of water.

"I've been working very hard to ignore... sadness," Jane said in a quiet voice. "But now that you're asking me questions, I guess I have to relive that day."

"You see, this is why I told you talking to her was a bad idea," Drew said, his lips set in a straight line.

"The real reason is you don't want her to find out what a horrible fiancée you were to my sister," Jane said with an edge to her voice. "But everybody is going to find out, anyway."

"Well, it doesn't really matter anymore," Drew scoffed.

"Fine. If it doesn't matter, then we should tell Cora," Jane said, glaring at Drew.

"We don't need to go into that," Drew said, less confidently. "You could answer her questions without adding anything."

For a moment, Cora wondered whether she should bring up that she already knew about Trudy. Seeing how uncomfortable Drew looked, however, she thought better of it.

"Okay," Jane said, turning to Cora. "You wanted to know if I noticed anything strange when Aria passed."

Cora nodded.

"No, nothing at all," Jane said in a muted voice. "Early that morning, Aria messaged me on my comm, apologizing for holding us up, but she was running late. Later, at the spaceport, she stepped into the antigrav lift. I could see her alone as the lift drifted downward. Then she was screaming, banging on the lift, and then... She just... collapsed."

"Do you know why she was late?" Cora asked.

"Yes. She'd spent the night at a friend's house," Jane said. "Aria had overslept. Actually, the whole family overslept. That was a little strange, but I never got the chance to ask her about it."

"Did you and Aria talk to each other? I mean, with your minds?" Cora asked, furrowing her eyebrows.

"Normally, yes," Jane said, scratching her head. "It was strange she didn't reach out to me when she saw me on the first floor."

"Did Aria speak to you with her mind?" Cora asked, turning to Drew.

"No. You're right, that was strange," Drew said.

"Where were you and Drew at the time?" Cora asked.

"He was with me on the bottom floor," Jane said. "We had a clear view of the glass lift. Our eyes met for a moment, then she blinked and..."

Cora paused while Jane cleared her throat.

"Linus was on the top floor," Drew said with irritation. "I bet he followed her to the spaceport."

Jane nodded.

"Have you spoken to the family where Aria spent the night?" Cora asked.

"No," Jane sighed. "I've been completely absorbed with the funeral and dealing with the IPS."

"Would you give me their name?" Cora asked.

"Of course, it's the Meadcroft family," Jane said. "She is... was friends with Wilma Meadcroft. It would probably be best if you waited until after the funeral to talk to them, though."

"I'll wait," Cora said. "So far, there are two strange things. First, Aria and the entire Meadcroft family overslept. Second, she didn't communicate with you. The Readers I met in school usually communicated mentally several times a day. I'd imagine as sisters, it'd be the same with you two."

Jane nodded with a sad smile.

"What do you think happened to her?" Drew asked in a low voice.

"I can't think of anything so far," Cora said. "On another note, were you able to get a list of family members who'll be at the funeral?"

"Yes," Jane nodded as she activated her comm bracelet, creating a private floating screen that prevented Cora from seeing the contents. Jane scrolled on the screen and then waved her hand in front of it. A moment later, Cora's comm bracelet chimed, and she glanced at it, verifying the transfer.

"I'll take a look at it and also cross reference with the security vids," Cora said.

"How exactly do you have access to the security vids?" Drew asked, narrowing his eyes.

"I'm afraid I can't say," Cora said.

"She's hiding things from you," Drew said in a tense voice. "Jane, why are you dealing with her?"

"I think the real question is why am I dealing with *you*?" Jane said in a raised voice. "You've done nothing but obstruct efforts to find out what happened to my sister. What I can't figure out is why *you're* not interested in what happened to your soon to be wife. Did you even love her? Is that why you were cheating on her?"

Drew turned white as he gazed around the restaurant, as if wondering who had heard their conversation. Suddenly, he jumped to his feet and stormed out of the restaurant. He crossed paths with Brian, who was on his way in. A moment later, Brian walked up to the table.

"Hello," Cora said. "Have a seat."

"So, what did I miss? He seemed pretty upset," Brian said, pointing in the direction of the door and taking a seat.

"Oh, just Drew being Drew," Jane said. "He's upset. I reminded him he was cheating on my sister."

"Oh, yeah, I've heard about that," Brian said.

"How did you hear about that?" Jane asked, raising her eyebrows.

"Aunt Ferna," Brian said. "She always knows all the gossip."

"You're talking about Ferna Robertson, of course." Jane said, scrunching her face in embarrassment. "I didn't realize it was common knowledge."

"It's probably not common knowledge," Cora said. "My Aunt Ferna has a way of finding things out very early. It's like she's a secret agent or something," Cora said with a lopsided smile.

"I'm sorry I'm late," Brian said. "Did I miss the conversation?"

"Yeah, we're nearly done here," Cora said. "I can fill you in on what we discussed."

All three stood and meandered to the front.

"Oh, I forgot to ask," Cora said. "Would you send me the death report on your sister whenever it's available?"

"Yes, of course," Jane said. "The IPS will send it to my parents. I'll ask them about it and have it forwarded to you."

Once they exited through the doors and onto the busy sidewalk, Cora glanced up at the clear Lunar City Dome. She gazed at the waning Earth phase against the black sky and stars.

"One more thing," Cora said. "Who benefits from your sister's passing?"

Jane turned slightly pink, which made Cora wonder about it. With so many people on the sidewalk, she still couldn't lower her shield.

"I'm actually not sure," Jane said without meeting Cora's eyes. "Probably a family member. I'll ask my parents."

Cora and Brian exchanged glances.

"Oh, I need to be someplace else," Jane said, glancing at her comm bracelet. "I'm meeting my mom for funeral preparations."

Jane gave Cora a quick hug and disappeared into the crowd.

Brian chortled.

"She really is a terrible liar," Cora said with a small-smile.

Cora, Aunt Ferna and Brian took one of the underground floating trains to a private spaceport. Their formal clothing blended well with the handful of other Askovs in the train car with them. After a thirty-minute ride, the three of them emerged onto a platform. Standing next to the train, they spotted Benjamin, Omar, and his girlfriend, Irene.

"This is so exciting," Cora said with glee. She'd dressed in a formal, long black dress with a pale blue necklace and matching earrings. She'd also put her hair up in a chignon. "I've never taken a lunar crater tour."

"It's a little dull, my dear," Aunt Ferna said, wearing a sparkling gold gown. "I've taken two tours in the past, and the only thing that made it bearable was conversations with my friends."

"Oh, Ferna," Benjamin said with exasperation in a formal dark-gray jumpsuit. "As usual, you've missed the point." He turned to Cora. "The first thing you'll notice will be the beautiful shadowing on the landscape. The entire trip will be an experience."

"I kind of agree with Ferna on this," Omar, dressed in a navy-blue jumpsuit, said with a chuckle as Benjamin rounded on him.. "I understand you rock aficionados like diving into what could've caused the crater. What type of rock is this? Does that shadow look like an alien's head? But the rest of us think the whole thing is silly."

"Oh, Omar," Irene said with a playful smile. She wore a beautiful sage-green gown. "It's not that bad. I'm not into rocks either, but we're traveling on a space yacht. We'll have the highest quality of everything. I don't often get to experience something like this."

"And that's exactly what I mean," Aunt Ferna said. "It's the atmosphere of the space yacht and the friends you travel with. I love getting dressed in beautiful clothes and chatting and laughing with new friends you make on the way."

"Well, I can't wait to get started," Cora said, chuckling at their conversation.

The group meandered down a hall toward a security door. As they reached it, a floating, green and black, spherical robot emerged from it as it slid open. It announced their names and showed them into a plush gray and white lounge where they waited with several other Askovs.

"The Sea Draft Space Yacht is ready for boarding," the floating robot announced.

A crowd of well-dressed Askovs, many of whom Cora recognized, stood. They made their way up a gentle incline, through double-wide doors, and into the ship. Stepping onto the top floor of the ship, Cora marveled at the two-tier large, circular room surrounded by windows for almost three hundred and sixty degrees. The upper portion of the floor was a wide podium encircling the room's edge just under the windows. The lower floor section comprised the center portion of the floor covered in plush carpeting and included multiple dining tables of various sizes to accommodate parties of two to ten people.

The six of them made their way to their assigned table and took their seats. Cora sat between Brian and Aunt Ferna. Benjamin sat next to Brian, and Omar and Irene lowered into the two remaining seats. Their table, situated closer to the podium, would give Cora a wonderful view of the lunar landscape.

"Looks like we're finally moving," Benjamin said as the ship made its way down a tunnel. The lighting along the walls of the tunnel sped past them and a moment later disappeared as the space yacht slipped over the moon's surface. It moved like a hovercar on Earth, but Cora thought it wouldn't be as maneuverable. Hovercars were a form of transportation with no wheels that maneuvered through the air to convey people long distances.

"There's the quarter view of Earth," Cora said, craning her neck to peer at the windows behind. Turning to the direction the ship sailed, she furrowed her eyebrows. "I can't tell which direction we're going."

"I think it's north," Brian said, peering at the partial view of the landscape.

"Would you like something to drink, dear?" Aunt Ferna asked.

Cora shook her head.

"When do you think we can stand?" she asked, fidgeting like a child. "I want to see where we're going."

"You can stand now. I'll go with you," Benjamin said, chuckling at Cora's excitement. "I've never taken this tour before, either."

Cora and Benjamin stood, and Brian joined them.

"I'm coming too," Brian said as he reached out for Cora's hand. The two held hands, making their way to the upper floor just under the windows.

"Oh, this is a much better view of the landscape," Cora said with wide eyes. "Benjamin, you were right. The eerie shadows over the rocks and boulders make it seem as if something's moving. Maybe the moon has ghosts."

The three of them burst out laughing.

"Really?" Brian asked.

"This landscape is breathtaking," Cora said with a smirk. "Now I understand why there're so many images and vid captures of this landscape. Unfortunately, nothing compares to seeing it for yourself."

"Dinner will be available in five minutes," the floating robot announced as the three stood on the platform, admiring the view.

"What do you think?" Benjamin asked. "Should we head back?"

"Sure, I've been looking forward to lunar steak," Brian said, guiding Cora away from the windows. "Have you noticed that all the food here on the moon has a somewhat distinct taste? What causes that?"

"After four months, I don't notice anything anymore," Benjamin said.

"I definitely notice it. My eggs taste like the crafter cooked them in vegetable soup," Cora said. "It's not unpleasant, just unusual."

They reached the table and took their seats

"Aunt Ferna was telling me about a Seer," Irene said, turning to Aunt Ferna. "Have you met her yet?

"No, I still need to contact her," Aunt Ferna said.

Cora forced herself not to roll her eyes

"Would you like to come with me?" Aunt Ferna asked, glancing at Cora.

"You know what I think of them," Cora said with a frown. "They're only going to take your credits."

"They're not all bad," Aunt Ferna said, raising one eyebrow. "Some have a real ability. You haven't met the right one yet."

"So, who's this Seer?" Benjamin asked in a level voice as he shared Cora's opinion of them.

"Hilda, she's a real Seer," Aunt Ferna said. "My friend Kenna mentioned her several times. In fact, she uses Hilda to recommend business deals to her brother."

Benjamin and Omar tried but failed to stifle their laughter.

Irene and Aunt Ferna gazed at them with pinched faces.

"You shouldn't judge her when you've never met her," Aunt Ferna said. "She's helped the Yarmouth family double their credits."

"I've been to see her only one time," Irene said. "She helped me too. It was a personal matter, so I can't tell you, but Hilda is the real thing."

"You know, I think I'm ready to order," Brian said, exchanging a glance with Cora as he tried to change the topic.

"Yes, what's the special here?" Cora chimed in. "I'm kind of in the mood for something light with lots of crystallized vegetables."

They each made their selections from the meal crafter, and a moment later, their meals materialized on the table.

"There's something about the way they do chicken," Cora said after swallowing a bit. It was a mix of a tangy chicken rub and crispy flavorful vegetables. "It's so moist while the vegetables underneath stay crunchy."

"I don't know how they do that," Irene said. "I had that dish a few days ago in Lunar City, but the vegetables became mushy. This fish is crispy on the outside and moist on the inside. They must have a very advanced kitchen."

"I know the pantry made a perfect steak," Omar said.

Thirty minutes later, the space yacht reached the edge of the crater. It hovered for ten minutes, allowing those passengers interested to step onto the podium.

Cora, Brian, and Benjamin returned to the windows, gazing into the depths of the crater. Several passengers jostled them for a better view, but Brian held Cora's hand.

Then the ship began its slow descent. Cora surveyed the crater's walls, trying to absorb the varying gray stone that started lighter at the top and grew darker as the space yacht descended. She peered at the white spidery veins criss-crossing the darkening walls. Tiny shards of shiny rocks reflected dim lighting, adding to the eerie feeling as they floated downward.

"Can't wait to see what the bottom looks like," Cora said, giving Brian's hand a tight squeeze. Several other passengers pushed past them, trying to get a better view.

A moment later, they reached the bottom of the crater and the robot turned on the outside lights.

"Oh," Cora gasped. "Old lava flow. Look at the reflective rock outlining the flow. I think it's callenium. It's used in many devices because it perfectly reflects energy."

She stared at the crater's dark bottom that resembled a pot of black porridge that had been stirred by a giant and then frozen in mid-motion. The only thing missing was the stirring stick.

Cora turned to face Brian, giving him a broad grin. She leaned closer and mouthed a thank you. His eyes twinkled in response.

CHAPTER 8

After breakfast, Cora sat on the sofa of the suite wearing a powder blue top with matching pants. This time she had two floating screens surrounding her, and she used one to monitor Mystery Adventures. After verifying there were no issues, she started a vidchat with Steven while turning to the second screen to evaluate some information he had sent.

"Have you looked at the vids?" Steven asked.

"Yes, but I need some help with a few things," Cora said. "It seems Aria Spencer's private funeral took place yesterday."

"Yeah," he said. "You have a list of attendees."

"Your list only includes close members of the Spencer and Yarmouth families," she said. "There're no friends." Most of the time, the first funeral included immediate family members and close friends. Sometimes the family held a second, more public funeral for other family and friends.

"Strange, isn't it?" he said. "No friends."

"I'll ask Jane about that," she said, turning between his list on one screen and his image on another.

"Now my question is about the vids," she said, altering the screen with the list to a vid showing the crowds around the time Aria passed away.

"What's the problem?" he asked.

"I've studied all your vids," she said. "But I can't tell what you're trying to show me. It looks like a crowd of shocked people. Nobody on the funeral list, except Jane, was at the spaceport."

"Exactly," he said with a grim smile. "Don't you find that odd? Where's mom and dad? She was planning a week's long trip."

"I suppose," she said with hesitation. "I don't think my family would've seen me off on such a short trip, but they were a little odd."

"Perhaps," he said, turning his head when something chimed.

"But I got a good view of Drew, Jane, Porter, and Gavin," Cora said. "Linus would've been on the upper floor. Are there vids of that floor?"

"Yes," Steven said as he turned to a second chime. "I'll send that along to you, but right now,

I need to go." A moment later, his screen turned black.

Cora sent a message to Jane, letting her know about her conversation with Kenna, where she discussed the issue with Drew and Trudy. Kenna and the entire Yarmouth family wanted the marriage between Drew and Are and wouldn't have had a reason to harm her. But it helped eliminate suspects. She asked if her family had plans for a second funeral. Before ending her message, she asked for Linus and Porter's contact information.

She stood and stretched, ready for a break. She looked forward to meeting Brian for lunch.

"Must be running late," Cora said to herself and reached for her comm bracelet. It had been over ten minutes since Brian had said he would be here.

He rushed through the door out of breath.

"Sorry, I'm late," Brian said. "Got held up again with another client. But I'm ready if you are."

"Looking forward to it," she said. "Where're we going?"

"It's top secret," he said with a wink. "You'll have to trust me."

She chuckled.

"I want you to stay here," he said, giving her a quick hug. "No peeking." He stepped around her.

"What are you up to?" she asked with a giggle.

"I just need to get something," he said as his voice came from the other side of the room.

When he rejoined her, he had a gray bag slung over one shoulder.

"What's that?" Cora asked, stepping a little closer.

"Nothing for you to worry about," he said in a singsong tone. He wrapped one arm around hers and guided her out of the suite.

"You know you're terrible at keeping secrets," she said with a mischievous smile.

"I know, but this time I only have to hold out for ten minutes," he said in a mock serious tone. "I think I can do it."

"You sound like a little kid, trying to hide a piece of candy," she laughed. "Sometimes you can be so silly."

"I know. It's one of my redeeming qualities, right?" he replied.

They both laughed as they made their way to the antigrav lift. Taking the lift down to the first floor, they exited Athos Tower.

They dodged around people on the busy walkway that wrapped around Central Park. Following it into the park, Brian led Cora down a gravel path she hadn't noticed before.

"Oh, this is beautiful," Cora said. "Were these flowers in bloom the last time we were here?"

"Yeah," Brian said. "We're toward the end of their season, though. So, these are one of a few flowers blooming in the park."

"How do they simulate seasons here in Lunar City?" she asked.

"I don't really know," he said with a shrug. "It has something to do with varying the temperatures of the ground they're growing in. Also, at certain times of the year, you'll see specific plants hooded to maintain their desired moisture and temperature."

"I'd love to learn more about it," she said as her eyes lingered on the flowers.

"Where we're going, there won't be any flowers," he said. "But you'll see ferns, philodendrons, and... something else I've forgotten. Don't tell Mom."

They chuckled.

"I forgot your mom was also a gardener," she said. "So, there'll be no flowers... Does that mean our destination is the park? We're not walking through?"

"Oh," he said with a sheepish grin. "Okay, no more talking."

They took the winding path further into Central Park. The number of lush green plants increased, as did the moisture in the air.

"I've never been to this part of the park," she said, examining their surroundings. "I love these green ground cover plants next to our trail—kind of reminds me of home."

"Well, you're going to love our picnic area," he said.

"Picnic!" she said, turning to him. "Is that what you have in the bag?"

"Ah, I almost made it," he said in mock horror.

Cora laughed, and they linked arms again, continuing their walk.

As they rounded a bend in the path, Cora spied a metal table with two metal chairs nestled into a loose archway of Ficus plants that provided cover from passersby on the path. But it opened onto a bubbling stream on the other side of the table.

"Oh, this is beautiful," she said, stepping to the table, taking a seat, and peering at the creek.

"I thought you might enjoy eating here," he said with a broad grin. "Now onto the food." He placed the bag on the table and dragged out the food with a flourish. Soon the table supported two large covered platters, two smaller food boxes, and drinks.

Cora chuckled.

"This is roasted rosemary chicken on a bed of mashed potatoes," he said, removing the lid with a sweep. Specialized factories grew synthetic animal products, which Cora recognized on her plate. It was considered cleaner and more humane than farming animals.

Cora clapped, and he bowed.

"I have lemon salmon on a bed of rice," he said, removing his lid. "The drinks are tangy apricot, and the dessert is top secret."

"Another secret?" She giggled. "I'll guess while we're eating."

"So, what do you think?" he asked, taking his seat.

"I think it's perfect," she said with a broad grin.

She chewed on a bite of rosemary chicken, enjoying the piney marinade. Listening to the gurgling stream, she turned to her drink and took a sip of tangy apricot.

"Mmm... This is good," she said. "I didn't even know this drink existed here in Lunar City."

"Yeah, it's from one of those specialized farms," he said. "Many Originals build farmsteads and grow the highest quality foods. Then they create the most amazing food and drink combinations."

When Brian finished, he glanced at the two smaller boxes.

"Do you still want to guess?" he asked.

"It's something to do with chocolate," she said. "But I can't figure out what exactly."

Brian chuckled and opened the smaller containers, revealing two slices of very moist looking chocolate cake.

"That looks delicious," Cora said, taking a fork and cutting a small piece. "Wow, this is so moist."

"Isn't it, though?" Brian said around a mouthful of food, making it a little difficult to understand him.

"I'm sad to say I'm full, though," she said, putting down her fork. "I think I'll save this for later."

"Well, I think I'm going to have a few more bites," he said, digging into his cake again. After a few bites, he put down his fork.

"So, what's next?" she asked with a genial smile.

"So, I've been thinking about our problem," he said in a more serious tone. "You want to stay on Earth because you need to have input into Albright Corp. I understand. Albright maintains the troops that keep your mine safe from mine jumpers."

Cora took a sip of apricot juice, wondering where he was going with this.

"But we have this invention called faster-than-light communications," he said with a smirk. "It's the way you talk to your miners on Ganymede. It's the way the Spencers keep track of their mines on Mars."

Cora chuckled at his sarcasm. Faster-than-light communications or FTL Comm had been around for several generations. It facilitated communication between Earth, Mars, and Jupiter. This included the moons of all three planets and the asteroid belt between Mars and Jupiter. When everything worked well, it was like having a conversation with someone across the table. When it failed, the delays could be minutes to days long. But it was the tech that had helped her grandfather take control of Brimble mining when he won it gambling.

"All right, I see your point," Cora said. "I could stay in touch by maintaining good communication lines with Albright Corp and Mystery Adventures players. Also, I'd have improved contact with my miners on Ganymede just by being closer."

"It's not perfect," Brian said, his head bobbing up and down. "For critical communication, it can be dangerously slow."

"I'd considered the FTL Comm option," she said with furrowed eyebrows. "But there is something about the way your mom handed control over to Spencer Industries. I feel that it's important to maintain close contact with Jessica."

Brian frowned.

"But I'm willing to compromise," she added in a hurry, not wanting to shut down their conversation. "If I move to Mars, what would happen to Aunt Ferna?"

"Well, obviously she'd have to come with you," he said with an air of confidence.

"There's no such thing as 'obviously' when it comes to Aunt Ferna," she said. "She has many friends throughout Tymal and even here in Lunar City. People she's known her entire life. She won't walk away from all of that, and I don't blame her."

"Yeah, I can see that being a problem," he sighed. "I've often wondered why Dad's okay with leaving. He has my mom and many friends."

"This is the scenario that keeps running in my mind," she said, leaning forward. "A couple of years ago, the Spencers stole a mine from the Pendletons. It led to a skirmish, which caused them to draw troops away from smaller, less protected mines."

"Ugh, I was in charge of Albright Corp during that mess," he said.

"That's a case where I'd want to know what's happening, not with my mine, but with Jessica," she said in a steady voice. "She didn't withdraw troops from Brimble Mining, but I think it's too remote for now."

"I know," he said in a defeated voice. "I'm essentially leaving my mom and sister alone to fend off Jessica. But after the way, they both happily threw me away. I feel as if my dad is my only real supporter."

"You have me, too," she reached across the table and grasped his hand.

"You need a quicker response to defend against Jessica," he said with a half-smile. "I need an effective response to service my clients who need someone familiar with Martian law. There're so many intricacies with the law. They need help to know which to ignore and which to follow to the letter. It's extremely complicated, and I could help them better from Mars. I really feel that's my future."

"Tell me about your clients," Cora said as she felt a heaviness settling on her chest. "How is business going here in Lunar City?"

"At first, I developed several clients," Brian said. "At one point I had nine. It was sort of working because I told them I could use the FTL Comm between Lunar City and Anteros on Mars. But as time went by, I missed one or two extremely important meetings. This gave my client's competition an entry into negotiations. Once they started losing business to their rivals, one by one, they let me go."

"How many clients do you have now?" she asked, her heart breaking at his struggle.

"Three, I think," he said with a sigh. "One of them has already hinted that he'd rather use somebody based in Anteros."

"Three clients," she said. "You can't support yourself that way. What about going back to your old practice in Tymal?"

"On Earth, my legal expertise was not in the mining field," he said. "It was with marriage negotiations, buying and selling mine shares, and technology royalties. Just a hodge-podge of legal needs for Askovs. I was bored and had done that job for ten or twelve years."

"I only met you after Harold started teaching us to manage our mines," she said with a gentle smile. Harold Albright was Brian's uncle and taught Brian the ins-and-outs of mine management.

"When Uncle started teaching me, it opened new possibilities," he said with a grin. "Over the years, I've developed an expertise in all things mining. I even have a new certification. I want to go to Mars, but I'd really rather go with you by my side." He gave her hand a gentle squeeze.

"We need such different things. Is it even possible to compromise?" She asked as her heart sank.

"I think we can," Brian said with a half-smile.

"Let's keep talking," Cora said as a weight settled on her heart. "We'll come up with a solution
somehow. We just have to keep trying."

CHAPTER 9

Cora and Brian made their way past Central Park and through the Askov neighborhood until they reached the outer edge of Lunar City's major dome. Soon they both made it to the front door of the Rowley family. Victor and Glenda Rowley were members of the Albright Corporation with Cora, who was used to seeing them at their quarterly meetings on vidchat. Their home was a three-story high, gray, three-dimensional rectangle, and blended well with the neighboring homes.

As they stepped to the front door, they heard a voice.

"Coraline Brimble? Brian Ferris?" the home's AI asked.

"Yes, we're here to talk to Linus," Cora said.

"You are expected," the home's AI said as the door slid open.

They stepped inside and Cora grinned at the forest-like entryway. She inhaled the earthy scented air.

"Most Askov homes are like this." Brian chuckled. "Reminds me of Tymal."

Cora lowered her shield in small increments, trying to sense who was in the house. She sensed someone toward the center of the home and someone else two or three stories up. Since there weren't too many people in the home, she lowered her shield.

"Please follow the lighting in the floor," the home's AI said.

Cora and Brian strolled along a short hallway, which led them to the living room at the center of the home. Linus stood, ran a hand through his auburn hair, and dusted crumbs off of his shirt.

"Sorry, I kind of forgot you were coming today," Linus said, in a lunar drawl. "Come in and have a seat."

Cora and Brian lowered themselves to a soft faux leather sofa while he chose the neighboring one. He hurried to put his snacks in the recycling. "I'm sorry. Would you like something to drink? Tea. Coffee. Water?"

"No, I'm okay," Cora said.

"What were you eating when we walked in?" Brian asked.

"Sugar and cinnamon cookies," Linus said with a lopsided grin. "Want some?"

"If it's not too much trouble," Brian said, settling further into the sofa.

Linus pressed a button on the coffee table, and a moment later, three plates of cookies and cups of tea appeared on the table.

"Thanks," Brian said, reaching for a cookie. After taking the first bite, he turned to Cora. "You should try one."

Cora chuckled and shook her head. "We just ate."

"Mmm..." Brian said around a mouth full of cookie.

"Would you mind if I asked you a few questions?" Cora asked after they both finished their first cookies.

"I just want to say that I really hope you find out what happened to Aria," Linus said between bites of his second cookie. "I don't believe somebody that healthy would drop dead from a heart attack. So, ask me anything."

"What were you doing at the spaceport when Aria passed?" she asked.

"Oh, well... I was with Porter, who went to meet a friend," Linus said. "Uhmm, Gavin."

Cora sensed his lie, but she didn't need her abilities to tell he was lying. All the hesitations gave him away.

"You know, all I have to do is ask Porter," Cora said, surveying and examining his emotions. She sensed his deep well of sadness. Expecting him to be mourning his friend, she wasn't surprised at the grief, but there was another emotion mixed in.

"Look, I'm here to help you with whatever you need," Linus said with a scowl. "But what I was doing at the spaceport is none of your business."

"Let's continue," Cora said. "On the day Aria passed, did you notice anything unusual?"

Linus seemed to deflate as he exhaled and stared in the distance, thinking. Cora sensed his misery, which started at the mention of Aria.

"No," Linus replied in a quiet voice. "I didn't notice a thing. I wish I had noticed something, but everything looked normal."

"When I spoke to Jane, she mentioned Aria was running late," Cora said. "Do you have any idea why?"

"She was running late?" Linus asked. "Makes sense why she was rushing through the spaceport. I thought for a moment maybe she'd spotted me and she was trying to get away. So, I slowed down." He blinked, as if aware of what he'd said. "But I wasn't following her."

Cora and Brian exchanged glances.

"Did you often follow Aria?" Brian asked. "It's very important that you tell us the truth so that we can get to why Aria died."

"Okay, sometimes I followed her," Linus said, frowning. "But not very often, and when she asked me to stop, I stopped."

"Why did you follow her that day?" Cora asked, leaning forward a little, concentrating as she tried to understand the depth of his emotions.

"Well... I don't know." Linus shrugged. "I just... I don't know. I can't tell you why I followed her that day."

Cora sensed he was telling the truth. He had been in love with her. The heartbreak and medley of love, friendship, and longing made that clear. He was in love with somebody engaged to be married to somebody else.

Were those emotions enough to kill her? Cora wondered.

"Can we back up a little? How long have you known Aria and Jane?" Cora asked.

"Oh, that. We grew up together," Linus said, relaxing into the sofa. "We met when we were all teens. Well, Jane was younger. She was a little kid sister who kept following us. But the rest of us hung out together because we shared the same private tutors. There are no schools in Lunar City to help develop Askovian abilities."

"So, you met after classes?" Brian asked, taking his third cookie.

"We usually played games at Porter's house," Linus said. "We also went swimming at Aria's house, or worked on our clippers in the garage downstairs."

"Clippers?" Brian said, leaning forward. "Do you race them?" Clippers were highly maneuverable, one-person spaceships.

"We used to," Linus said. "But we outgrew them."

Cora sensed his lie, but there was something else. Maybe something connected to Aria. Maybe they'd bonded over building the tiny racing ships.

"You, Aria, Jane, and Porter spent time together?" Cora asked. "Anyone else?"

"Drew," Linus sighed. "I forgot Drew. He never contributed much to the activities."

Cora sensed a ripple of bitterness.

"I find it interesting that all of you were at the spaceport at the same time," Cora said. "That couldn't have been a coincidence."

"It wasn't planned—there's only one shuttle from Earth a day," Linus said with a shrug. "Aria and Drew had been planning to take a vacation back to Earth for months. It makes sense Jane would accompany her sister—they were close. Porter is at the spaceport frequently because his investors are on Earth. And... you know why I was there."

Linus stood and paced to the faux fireplace and leaned on the mantel. He studied an image of a field of flowers taken on Earth.

"Look, I've told you everything I know," Linus said, turning to Cora and Brian. "Do you have any more questions? Because otherwise I have some things I could be doing."

"Do you have any theories about what happened to Aria?" Cora asked as she stood.

"No, of course I don't," Linus frowned. "I'd have told you that to begin with." He sighed. "The IPS thinks a Reader killed her with a suggestion. They've interviewed Jane twice already just because she's a Reader."

"What do you think about that theory?" Cora asked, stepping closer to Linus. "A Reader could have put an idea in her head that would cause her brain to send a message to her heart to stop?"

"I've heard of that happening," Linus said, furrowing his eyebrows. "But it only happens in the Casino Dome because of organized crime. I've never heard of it happening among the Askov."

"What do you think about the idea that Jane is the Reader who killed her sister?" Cora asked.

Linus chuckled.

"Is it even a possibility?" Brian asked, climbing to his feet.

"Absolutely not," Linus said with finality. "If you'd known them when Aria was alive, you'd agree with me."

"Out of curiosity, why do you carry a blaster?" Cora asked, changing the direction of their conversation.

"Oh, that," Linus said with a lopsided smile. "I'm planning a trip in a few weeks, and I'll need to protect myself."

"Where—" Cora said.

"Linus, Linus?" a higher pitched, lilting voice called interrupting Cora. "Where are you, dear? Oh, there you are."

A woman in her fifties glided into the living room. She was a tall, striking redhead, and she wore a deep-green dress.

"Mom, this is Cora Brimble and Brian Farris," Linus said.

"Oh, yes. I know Cora and Brian," Glenda said with a genial smile. "I think Ferna is planning a get-together for dinner. We'll talk then. Right now, I'm off to the stores." She twirled and paced out of the room.

"Well, thank you for your help," Cora said. "Can I contact you if I have more questions?"

"Yeah, sure," Linus said, staring into the distance again.

Cora and Brian turned and stepped toward the front door. Once they were outside, they walked toward the Lunar Cafe.

"What did you think of Linus?" Brian asked.

"Well, he's lying about something," Cora said.

"I think he was at the spaceport to declare his love to Aria before she got married," Brian said with a thoughtful expression.

"That might be it," Cora said. "But we also have a few new strange things."

"What's the story behind him wearing a blaster?" Cora said. "Even his friends seemed surprised."

"Why were all five friends at the spaceport at the same time?" Brian asked. "And why do they think it was a coincidence?"

"Maybe somebody's in the background manipulating things," Cora said in a low voice.

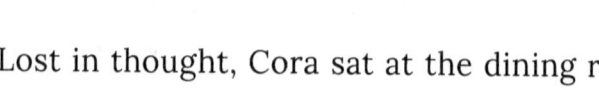

Lost in thought, Cora sat at the dining room table, staring at an apricot teacake and a cold cup of coffee. She thought of the long list of things she could do, but somehow couldn't muster the energy to get started.

Aunt Ferna bustled into their suite with a pile of packages.

"Afternoon, my dear," Aunt Ferna said with a bright smile. "I thought you and Brian had plans this afternoon."

"We did," Cora sighed. "But a client changed his meeting at the last minute, and Brian had to rush off."

"Well, that's too bad," Aunt Ferna said, dropping her packages on the sofa and joining Cora at the dining table. "What was the plan for this afternoon? Maybe the two of us could go?"

"We were going to the rock museum," Cora said. "They have an exhibit on non-native moon rocks. There're quite a few from Mars."

Aunt Ferna wrinkled her nose.

"Don't worry, I won't make you go." Cora giggled.

Aunt Ferna wiped her forehead with exaggerated relief.

They laughed together.

"I think I'll have tea and cake," Aunt Ferna asked.

"Now, now, don't worry," Aunt Ferna said. "Brian can take you tomorrow."

"I know," Cora said with a half-smile.

"Benjamin mentioned there's a chance Brian would join him and Omar on their journey to Mars," Aunt Ferna said.

Cora gazed at her aunt, wondering what she could add that wouldn't make her more depressed.

"Oh, I see," Aunt Ferna said. "I really don't think Brian is going with his dad. Everyone can see how much he cares for you."

"Maybe… I don't want to interfere in their relationship," Cora said. "Going to Mars will give them a chance to spend a lot of time together, especially now that Benjamin is retired."

"True..." Aunt Ferna said, staring off into space. "But I have a hunch he's not going anywhere."

"What about you?" Cora asked. "Aren't you home a little early?"

"Well, yes," Aunt Ferna said. "Kenna had a full day of plans for the two of us. There's a lady's auxiliary, a tour, and another afternoon tea. But I wanted to spend some time relaxing. I've been busy almost every day since we arrived in Lunar City."

"Relaxing is good," Cora said. "I think I'll refresh my coffee." She selected a button on the meal crafter, which reheated her coffee.

Aunt Ferna selected a strawberry teacake and a warm cup of tea, and they ate.

"Oh, I wanted to tell you about my morning," Aunt Ferna said, wiping her mouth. "Kenna and I went to visit Hilda."

This time Cora rolled her eyes

"I know you don't think much of Seers, but listen," Aunt Ferna said in a determined voice. "Hilda and I met about Oliver. I asked if he was safe and happy, and I wanted to know any information she could sense about him. The EGS stopped replying to my inquiries after our first hearing."

"What did she say?" Cora asked, trying to be polite.

"She told me Oliver was dead," Aunt Ferna said, the last with the quavery voice.

Cora stood and walked to her aunt's side of the table. She embraced her aunt in a warm hug and took the seat next to her.

"I'm not sure you should take the word of a Seer," Cora said in a gentle voice. "Surely the EGS would've contacted you if Oliver had passed away."

"Not if they'd caused his death," Aunt Ferna said with a scowl. "I want to tell you something I've never told anyone else." She paused, gathering her thoughts. "Sometimes I get a hunch, an idea, or a feeling about something. Most of the time, it's true."

"I've noticed that, and mentioned it to Brian," Cora said, reaching for Aunt Ferna's hand and giving it a squeeze. "I think you're a Feeler, but your abilities aren't as strong as Mom's. That caused grandpa to dismiss your training, otherwise I'll bet you could have developed or even controlled them."

"Well, I don't know about being a Feeler," Aunt Ferna said, turning a little pink. "Sometimes I just know things. Strange right?"

"I don't think it's strange at all," Cora said. "Like you, Brian also gets hunches. Many times, they're right. It could be that you both have very good hunches. In fact, when I mentioned my idea to Brian, he felt he was a Seer."

Aunt Ferna guffawed.

"Don't laugh," Cora said, crossing her arms with a half-smile. "Brian is not a Seer."

"That'd be your worst nightmare." Aunt Ferna chuckled.

"Well, four and a half months ago exactly, I sensed Oliver passed away," Aunt Ferna said as a frown covered her face. "I don't know why I felt that way, but somehow I knew it was absolutely true."

"I'm so sorry," Cora said, giving her aunt a gentle hug.

Aunt Ferna wiped her eyes

"Hilda sensed Oliver had died due to some experimentation," Aunt Ferna said. "The EGS or military or both conducted many on him."

Cora nodded as new thoughts crossed her mind. What if the line between Seers and Feelers was imprecise? Our way of understanding all special abilities could be wrong. What if some Askovs could have more than one ability?

"The last thing Hilda told me was Oliver would be avenged," Aunt Ferna said with a scowl. "The EGS, IPS, and military will disintegrate in less than ten years."

"That sounds like a scary future," Cora said with a shiver.

"It's not too different from the way the IPS operates now," Aunt Ferna said. "A couple of years ago, the Spencers stole a Pendleton mine. The IPS should have prevented that, but Evan Pendleton had to rely on his own personal armed forces."

"Good point," Cora said. "It's the reason I stay so active with the Albright Corp. Our mine is too small to afford its own army."

"But I've heard many rumors about the EGS disintegrating for years now," Cora said. "Don't you think Hilda is simply repeating what she's heard?"

"Of course, I've heard the same rumors too," Aunt Ferna said. "But she corroborated my feelings about Oliver."

"Knowing that Oliver is dead is worrying," Cora said with a frown. "What if she has ties to some sort of organization? What if she's a secret Reader and scanned your mind?"

"Or what if she has the ability to see into the past and future?" Aunt Ferna asked. "I think you need to open your mind to other possibilities."

Cora shrugged.

"I can't imagine that ability being real," Cora said. "Meeting Etta confirmed my suspicions."

Aunt Ferna nodded, staring down at her tea growing cold.

Cora gave her a comforting hug. Even though she had never liked Oliver, she wracked her mind, trying to think of something to ease her aunt's loss.

CHAPTER 10

Cora and Brian walked through Central Park to two different meetings. Brian strode to meet a client who insisted on additional meetings to discuss a legal issue. Cora paced to meet with Agent Taylor.

"I don't like you meeting Taylor by yourself," Brian said with a frown.

"I've met with the EGS before, and at least the last time, it turned out... okay," Cora said with furrowed eyebrows. She wore a tan formal shirt with a conservative black skirt, hoping to fit in with the IPS agent's expectations. "Most of the time, that agent was reasonable and even helpful."

"That's what bothers me," he said. "We don't know anything about this one. Is she insane like the first agent who arrested you or reasonable like the last one?

"I see—" she said.

"I also haven't asked around yet," he said, interrupting her. "Wish I could get out of this appointment, but my client is frantic right now."

"What's the problem?" she asked, trying to distract him.

"He's having pretty extensive legal issues on Mars," he said with a sigh. "A different set of attorneys are helping him there. He wants me to help protect his business ventures on Earth. He's done everything to separate all three of his businesses, but his legal issues from Mars are spilling over into other areas."

"Sounds messy," she said. "I don't envy you."

They passed through the park and onto a busy walkway that looped around it. They surveyed the business division full of multi-story buildings. Brian gave her a peck on the cheek, a gentle smile, and turned, veering to the right toward a tall blue and white building.

Cora stood for a moment, gazing at his back before she gave herself a mental shake. She paced across the busy walkway and stepped into the tallest building in the business sector. It was an odd combination of gray with yellow stripes. She supposed they wanted potential customers to notice them, as the two colors clashed a little. Stepping through the front doors, a floating gray and yellow robot greeted her. She remained shielded from so many people in the building.

"Good morning Coraline Brimble," the robot said. "You have an appointment with Agent Taylor. Please follow the lighting in the corridor. She's in conference room number five on the left."

Cora nodded and followed the pulsating lights in the floor. The building, like many Askov homes, was decorated with green leafy plants that humanized the otherwise harsh gray walls and taupe carpet. As she reached the conference room door, it slid open, and she spotted Agent Taylor. She was an average height, maybe in her thirties, with straight black, shoulder-length hair.

"Morning, Ms. Brimble," Agent Taylor said, standing up. "Please have a seat. She gestured to a seat on the other side of the table from her.

"Morning," Cora said, taking the seat.

"Do you know why you're here today?" Agent Taylor asked, activating a screen embedded into the table.

"I suppose this has to do with Aria Spencer's death," Cora said, straining to see anything on Agent Taylor's screen, but she'd set it to private.

"I've been reading your history with the EGS," Agent Taylor said. "How did you end up at the scene of two murders earlier this year?"

"Is this really what you want to know?" Cora asked, feeling irritation bubbling up from her stomach. "I thought it was urgent to find a murderer before too much time passed. Shouldn't you be asking me questions about Aria Spencer?"

Looking up from the screen, Agent Taylor set her lips in a straight line. One of her jaw muscles jumped as she leaned back in her chair and crossed her arms.

"You didn't know Aria Spencer," Agent Taylor said. "There's no reason to ask you about her."

"So, why did you want me?" Cora asked with furrowed eyebrows.

"I understand you've been helping Jane Spencer," Agent Taylor said. "Are you aware she's our prime suspect?"

"Well, yes. She mentioned something about that," Cora said in a level voice. "But I think you've got the wrong person. Jane loved her sister."

"Have you heard of one lover killing another over a spat?" Agent Taylor said with a smirk.

"Yes, of course," Cora said. "In this case, I don't see a motive."

Agent Taylor raised an eyebrow at her words, but said nothing.

"Do you know something that could help me?" Cora asked, knowing Agent Taylor wouldn't answer.

"That's the point," Agent Taylor said in a firm voice. "You shouldn't be investigating. That's our job."

"But on Earth, when I conducted a few inquiries in parallel with the EGS, it helped," Cora said. "You might benefit from any information I find."

The agent seemed to think it over for a second. "Very well. What have you found so far?" she asked, her eyes boring into Cora's.

"Well, not too much," Cora said with hesitation. "I've only spoken to Jane, Linus, and Kenna Yarmouth. I didn't learn anything from them." She paused for a moment. "Except I felt Jane and Linus were hiding something from me, but I'll need more time to figure it out."

Agent Taylor chuckled

"I can't believe Captain Donaldson praised you so much," Agent Taylor said. "You've provided no helpful information at all." She rested her elbows on the table. "Listen. Stop all your inquiries, now. Best case, they'll interfere with our investigation. In the worst case, the killer could target you next."

Even though she tried to ignore Agent Taylor's words, the mention of the killer made Cora shiver.

"I understand I could be in danger," Cora said, doing her best to remain calm. "Having conversations with a few of her friends and family is all I intend. Also, I report everything I find to Jane. I could let you know what I find as well, if you're interested."

"Please don't waste my time," Agent Taylor said the last word in a raised voice. She popped to her feet, waving a hand over the screen. Faux wood covered the screen as she stalked out. Cora gazed about the empty room and the door where Agent Taylor had exited.

Did she really invite me down here just to tell me to stop? She could've sent me a vidchat, Cora thought, pursing her lips with irritation as she made her way out of the room.

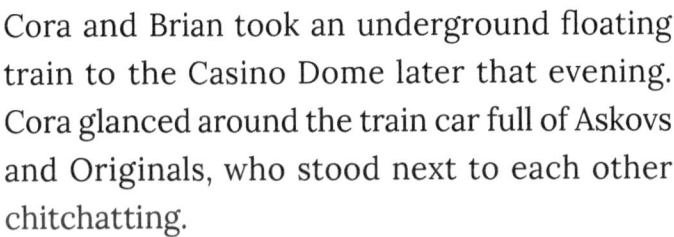

Cora and Brian took an underground floating train to the Casino Dome later that evening. Cora glanced around the train car full of Askovs and Originals, who stood next to each other chitchatting.

What makes these Askovs and Originals cordial to each other? she thought.

"I see everyone is friendly when they're heading to the Casino Dome," Brian said with a smirk. He wore a casual peach top and black pants. "Maybe a common activity makes them drop their guard."

"I suppose so, but it's strange," Cora said, wearing an evening red dress. "Usually I hear of camaraderie between people who are going into battle, but this is just gambling."

"This is about the dream of winning a fortune," Brian said. "It can feel like battle, but it's the sort of thing that creates addicts."

"I see," Cora said, catching a few people peering at her and then glancing away. "I think they are still afraid of me, though."

"Try to ignore them," Brian said, glancing at the other passengers.

A moment later, the train came to a stop and a sea of people flowed out of the doors. Brian and Cora followed behind. The antigrav lifts filled quickly. But most people took the wide, shallow staircase next to the lifts. Cora and Brian drifted with the crowd, joining a wide, busy pathway.

Cora stared wide-eyed at the tall buildings filling the dome. Each building housed a single casino and displayed bright, flashy advertisements against their walls. They followed a winding walkway connecting all the casinos.

Though she had shielded her mind even before entering the train, Cora still experienced some sensory overload. Several human entertainers darted among the crowds, trying to entice passersby to enter each casino. Floating robots emitted noisy advertisements while the flashing lights from the buildings made it so that she couldn't tell where to focus. The noise and lights slowed Cora down as her brain tried to process it all.

"This way," Brian said, wrapping his arm around hers and guiding her along the walkway. They passed the entrance to a building with two doors, covered in dots and tilted at forty-five degrees away from each other. Another building showed a woman jumping up and down as gold coins tumbled over her. They passed two more buildings, Brian guiding her toward one with walls, which resembled a series of waterfalls flowing from the roof all the way to the ground. It was a hologram that also included people taking the waterfall from the top all the way to the bottom while screaming and laughing.

Once she stepped inside, it wasn't any quieter, and the lights were even brighter. A woman appeared in a revealing top and a short skirt. The entire outfit flashed with red and green lights.

"Would you like to gamble?" the flashing woman asked.

"No, we have reservations at the restaurant," Brian said.

"Of course, it's this way," the flashing woman gestured to a hallway. "Please follow the lighting in the floor."

Brian nodded and led Cora down a narrower walkway. She breathed a sigh of relief to be away from the lights and noise. She turned to him with a gentle smile as they stood at the entrance to the dark and quiet restaurant.

"Better?" he asked.

"Yeah, thank you," she said and took in the restaurant's atmosphere. The earthy smell of real dirt, green plants, and faint flower aromas made her feel at home. "I think I'm going to like it here."

"Dad recommended this place," he said. "But I've never been here before."

"How many are in your party?" a green and black floating robot asked.

"We're here to meet Benjamin Farris," Brian said.

"Of course, please follow me," the robot said and floated around several tables as it wound its way to the very back of the restaurant. There they met Aunt Ferna, Benjamin, Omar, and Irene. Benjamin and Omar stood.

"Are we late, Dad? Brian asked.

"No, no. Have a seat," Benjamin said. "The three of us got here early because we were gambling." He gestured to Omar and Irene. "I'm not sure how Aunt Ferna got here so early."

"I had lunch in another casino with some friends," Aunt Ferna said and turned a little pink. "We may have done a bit of gambling."

"You've been having fun while Brian and I worked," Cora said with a broad smile. "I see how it is." She took her seat and Brian, Benjamin, and Omar took theirs.

"I worked too," Aunt Ferna said and leaned closer to Cora. "I've learned something that'll help your investigation."

"Really! What is it?" Cora asked.

"Aria left a will," Aunt Ferna said in a low voice, although everyone at the table could hear her.

"Surprising Jane didn't mention it," Cora said. "Who's the beneficiary?"

"Jane, of course," Aunt Ferna said. "That's the real reason the IPS is so focused on her. It doesn't hurt that she's a Reader as well."

"Now I know why she didn't mention it," Cora said, shaking her head. "I suspect she's still innocent, but the lying won't help her against the IPS."

"It also explains why Jane asked for your help the day after her sister's murder," Brian said. "The IPS suspected her, and *she* needed your help."

"Now, now," Benjamin said. "We're supposed to be enjoying this evening, not working."

"This restaurant is beautiful," Cora said, trying to change the subject. "I love the forest theme and the air feels so warm and moist."

"I'm not a big fan of the humidity anymore," Irene said. "It's not uniformly spread through Lunar City. Also, it's an adjustment when I come across it in foyers and restaurants. On the other hand, I've never had such a severe case of dry skin since moving here."

Irene and Aunt Ferna tittered.

"I know what you mean about dry skin," Omar said. "I still prefer the moist air. Maybe I've lived on Earth for too long."

They each took turns ordering from the meal crafter, and a moment later, their meals materialized on the table.

"I understand from Ferna you're looking into Aria Spencer's murder." Benjamin said.

Cora nodded as she chewed a bite of steak.

"First, I want to say, please be careful," Benjamin said. "After all, somebody was murdered."

Cora took a sip of her water. "I don't want to put myself in danger," she said. "I only promised to help Jane by talking to some friends and family."

"Of course," Benjamin said. "The second thing I want to mention is it seems the IPS thinks the murderer could be a Reader. Many of these casinos employ Readers. They claim it's to keep us from stealing from them, but really, it's helping the casinos keep as many credits as possible."

"I thought we weren't supposed to be working," Brian smirked.

"And we're not going to," Benjamin said. "Instead, we're going to enter the casino and play games." He turned to Cora. "How do you intend to investigate a Reader?"

"I wasn't planning to," Cora said with a shrug. "Sensing a Reader in this environment would be impossible for me. But I'm open to walking around. Maybe something will catch my eye."

"I think tracking a stranger who's a Reader is too dangerous," Brian said. "I have no idea how Oliver used his Feeler abilities here."

"There are private gambling rooms," Irene said. "They'd have a limited number of people in the room, but you'd have to bring a pile of credits to play."

"One reason I suggested we have dinner here is this place is well known for its Readers," Benjamin said. "When we walk through the gambling floor, you should be able to spot them. They're the ones in formal black jumpsuits looking very menacing." He chuckled. "I don't know why the casino doesn't disguise them better."

"They employ more than one?" Cora asked.

"Yes, it makes sense," Benjamin said. "One Reader can't keep track of hundreds of people at the same time."

Cora nodded, and the conversation turned to Lunar City politics.

"I think the Lunar City Council should abolish these casinos," Aunt Ferna said with a frown. "They're the reason my Oliver got into trouble."

"But Aunt, you gamble for fun with your friends," Cora said with a raised eyebrow.

"That's different, we're just having fun," Aunt Ferna said, waving her hands and dismissing Cora's words. "I worry about the people who come here and get trapped in this life."

Several replies raced through Cora's mind, and she had to look away and force herself not to reply. Oliver had been in plenty of trouble before he fled to Lunar City.

"You know they'll never get rid of gambling," Benjamin said, chuckling. "The Casino Dome alone brings in three-quarters of the revenue that supports Lunar City. Spencer Industries and a few other businesses bring in the remaining amount. The council won't do anything to disrupt that. In fact, that's how I know they'll go through a lot of trouble to find Aria Spencer's murderer.

After chatting for a few more minutes, they stood to leave the restaurant and entered the casino gambling floor. The bright lights and loud sounds made Cora uncomfortable again, and she thought about leaving. Brian again wrapped his arm around hers and gave her hand a little squeeze.

"I think if you walk through once, we can leave without my dad complaining," Brian said. "Will that work for you?"

Cora nodded with a faint smile and stepped into the gambling area. She strolled past four rows of floating gambling machines. They all promised huge riches to the people sitting in front of the colorful screen with their eyes glued as they played. Ambling past a series of tables, she surveyed the sets of six to eight people who played a game with rectangular, colorful blocks. She didn't recognize the game, but knew the colored blocks represented a certain amount of credits.

Cora felt something pressing on her mind. She glanced around and found a thin blonde woman with a tight ponytail glaring at her. Realizing she must be a Reader trying to invade her mind, Cora glanced at her clothing. Just as Benjamin promised, the woman was dressed in a man's formal jumpsuit. With plenty of experiences dealing with pushy Readers, Cora defended herself with little effort as she shielded her mind.

"How do you feel?" Cora asked.

"What do you mean?" Brian said. "It's very loud in here."

"Somebody's trying to push into my mind," she said. "And it occurred to me, they're probably doing it to you."

"If they are, I can't feel anything," he said with a shrug. "But it makes me feel uneasy. Let's hurry and leave this place."

Cora steered Brian away from the blonde ponytail, but as they rounded the next table, a tall, dark-haired man caught her eye. She sensed his gentle pushing against her mind. But it stopped when she turned to examine him. He shifted from foot-to-foot and strolled away.

"I think I'm ready to go," Cora said with a sigh. "It's tiring being here, and realistically, I can't do any investigating. So far, I've found the Readers in Lunar City are intrusive and just plain rude. If Jane wants to learn anything about the Readers, she can come here herself."

"They made their way to another table where Benjamin, Omar, and Irene played with multi-colored triangular pieces. All three held an alcoholic drink in their hands while they played their game.

"Where is Aunt Ferna?" Cora asked, raising her voice over the noise.

"She ran into a friend," Benjamin said and waved a hand in the general direction of the floating machines. "She's over there some-where."

"Dad, Cora and I are leaving," Brian said in a raised voice.

"Already! You just got here," Benjamin said with a frown.

"I know, but I find this place a little over-whelming." Brian said. "It's the noise and the lights."

Cora felt grateful that Brian covered for her. She wouldn't want to explain how overwhelmed she felt in a place like this.

"We're still having breakfast tomorrow morn-ing, right?" Benjamin asked with a broad smile.

"Of course, Dad. See you in the morning," Bri-an said as he patted his dad's shoulders.

As the two of them stepped out of the casi-no, they ran into Aunt Ferna talking to Glenda, Linus's mom. Cora recognized the tall, striking redhead right away.

"I'm surprised to see you again so soon," Cora said with a genial smile.

"You must be wondering what I'm doing at a casino," Glenda said with a nervous laugh.

"Not at all, my dear," Aunt Ferna said with a chuckle. "We all need time to simply have fun."

"Yes, well..." Glenda glanced at something further into the casino. "I was heading inside." She turned to Cora and Brian. "It was good to see you both." She turned and shuffled onto the casino floor.

"What was that about?" Brian asked with a half-smile.

"Maybe it's time we all head home," Aunt Ferna said.

The three of them turned to the busy walkway and made their way to the underground train.

As they reached the entrance to the train's platform, her shoulders relaxed, and she took a deep breath.

I've never been so happy to leave a place, Cora thought.

CHAPTER 11

"When are we supposed to meet Porter again?" Brian asked, stepping out of his bedroom.

"In about an hour," Cora said, sitting on the gray and white sofa. She swallowed the last of her coffee. "It's a short walk away."

"Do you know what you're going to ask him?" he asked, pacing toward her.

"I only want a general sense of who he is," she said. "Getting a better understanding of his relationship with Aria might help. I don't have any specific ideas yet."

"Sounds good," he said, plopping down next to her on the sofa. "What are your plans for the rest of the day?"

"I think I'll spend some time looking through Mystery Adventures' messages," she said with a shrug. "A couple of error messages came up that I noticed the game's AI hadn't addressed. If there's time, I might do some programming this afternoon."

He stared at Cora's empty cup on the coffee table.

"What do you have planned?" she asked, sensing his disturbance.

"I'm going to meet a client," he said with a sigh. "Remember, I mentioned one of them wanted to fire me because I didn't have better contact with Anteros?"

Cora nodded.

"Well, I think we've reached a small compromise," he said. "I just have to contact the legal team every Martian cycle, about twenty-four and a half hours. I also need to contact his legal team on Earth about once a week."

"Do you even have enough to discuss every day?" she asked with raised eyebrows.

"Unfortunately, yes," he scowled. "It looks like somebody's going after his business. I have my suspicions but..."

"Can't discuss it?" she asked. "Understand. I only wanted to know if you could squeeze in a tour, but I think we're both booked."

Brian's comm bracelet chimed, and he launched a vidchat. A moment later, a floating screen appeared above his wrist.

"Hugo, what's going on?" he asked.

Cora couldn't see the man on the screen, as it was private.

"I'm sorry, man, but I think I'm going to let you go," Hugo said in a downcast voice.

"No, no," Brian said, jumping to his feet. "I understand what you're trying to accomplish with each of your businesses and have plans that can help you." Desperation shaded his words. "Let's talk. I'm sure we can work something out."

"Can you come to my office now?" Hugo replied.

Brian glanced at Cora, who nodded her approval.

"Of course, I'll be there in ten minutes," Brian said.

"I'm so sorry, Cora," he said, closing the floating screen. "Is there any way you can reschedule with Porter?"

"Yes, talk to Hugo," she said. "I'll contact Porter."

Brian gave her a grim smile as he stalked out of the suite.

Cora launched a vidchat with her comm bracelet, creating a floating screen. A moment later, Porter appeared.

"Hi, Porter," Cora said.

"Hello, is something wrong?" Porter asked.

"Not wrong precisely. There's a little snag," she said. "Brian can't make our meeting this morning. Can we delay it until the afternoon?"

"No. I've got a huge long line of meetings," he said. "I can only meet this morning. Are you sure you can't meet right now? It might be several days before we get to talk."

"Well…" she said, furrowing her eyebrows. She remembered her promise not to meet anyone alone. And then a thought crossed her mind. "Would you mind if we met at the Lunar Bakery instead of your office?"

"Oh, that's not a problem at all," he grinned. "In fact, I think I'm overdue for one of their chocolate teacakes. Can you get there in ten minutes?"

"I'm a little further away," she said. "I can be there in fifteen."

"Not a problem," he said. "I'll see you there in fifteen minutes."

Cora's floating screen turned dark. Then she selected a few symbols and launched a vidchat with Brian. But he didn't answer. Instead, she sent him a message letting him know about meeting Porter at the Lunar Bakery.

She reflected on her uneasy feeling of going against the agreement she'd made with Brian. Hoping he'd understand, she planned to explain everything to him. Their relationship had changed—it wasn't her fending for herself. Brian cared about her, and now she needed to make reasonable compromises.

Maybe I'm overthinking things, she thought.

Cora walked through the front doors of the Lunar Bakery for the first time. The smell of warm bread settled over her like a cozy blanket. A giant smile spread across her face as she inhaled. She decided this was her second favorite place in all of Lunar City, just behind Central Park. Glancing to the left, her eyes scanned rows of fresh baked bread, and a round blue robot placed them in a delivery shoot as new orders poured in. She made a mental note to have some sent to her suite.

When she turned to the right, her eyes found the seating area where delicious coffee aromas wafted into the air. It was the perfect combination. Porter caught her attention with a wave and a charming smile. As she strolled toward him, he stood.

"Cora. How've you been?" Porter said, standing.

"Fine," Cora said, taking a seat across from him.

Porter put his empty plate in the recycling and took a sip of coffee.

"I'm a little amazed that so many people know who I am," Cora said. "Originals are afraid of me, and Askovs know about me and some even look up to me. What's going on?"

"Oh, well, that I can explain," he replied. "There is a database compiled by Originals that keeps track of all Askovs. They keep it updated. Since you're a visitor here, they've added you. I'm not sure how they dig up all your information though."

"Can I see the database?" she asked.

"Yes, it's public," he said, activating his comm bracelet. "That's actually a bit of a problem. Sometimes they put private information in the database." A floating window appeared over the bracelet, and he maneuvered it between them. After selecting a few buttons, an extensive list appeared on the screen. A simple search later, and Cora stared at her name, family members, friends, school information, and even more detail about her abilities.

"That's disturbing," she said. "It's quite accurate. Even the information about Oliver is right."

"Even I'm in the database," he said, scrolling to his name. "I'm not Askovian, but I was born into an Askov family of Listeners. Some Originals think I'm safe and others are afraid of me."

"Wow, I wonder if this database will spread to Earth," she said, scrolling to Brian. "It's accurate... He comes from a family of Feelers and Readers, but he's not Askovian."

"Sometimes the information is not correct," he said with a chuckle. "Many years ago, the database reported I was worth one million credits. My cousins, who are all Listeners, are worth hundreds of millions of credits, but our side of the family is poor. Well... compared to my aunt and uncle."

"Did you correct the database?" Cora asked with a small smile.

"No! I needed investors," Porter chortled. "But someone corrected it, eventually."

"I'll order some coffee. Do you have any recommendations for pastry?"

"Everything's good. Choose something you like. You won't be disappointed."

Cora scrolled through the menu on the meal crafter and selected a cup of coffee and a Martian grown chocolate teacake.

"This cake is so moist," Cora said. "I love the dark chocolate flavor."

"It used to be my favorite, but I had the cinnamon teacake," Porter said.

"Would you mind if I ask you a few questions?" she asked.

"Anything. What would you like to know?" he asked.

"On the day Aria passed, did you notice anything unusual?" she asked.

"No, not really," he said. "I didn't know Aria and Drew were even there. I only wanted to pick up Gavin and discuss our next round of funding." He shook his head as if a disturbing thought had crossed his mind. "It's so strange to think. I was excited because it meant my business could limp along for another couple of years. At the same time Aria was dying."

"Did you see Aria, Drew, or Jane? I mean before?" she asked.

Porter shook his head.

"What happened after?" she asked.

"Somebody started screaming," he said with a quavery voice. He cleared his throat and continued. "I think it was Jane. When I looked where she pointed, I saw a crumpled heap on the floor of the antigrav lift. I didn't know that was Aria at first."

"How often does Gavin travel to Earth?" she asked.

"He goes maybe four to six times a year," he said. "Most of the time, he goes to the City of Tymal to meet our investors. He's an excellent programmer, and he has a way of making our investors like him. After our very first meeting with our investors, he banned me from meeting them anymore."

"Banned? Even though it's your own company?" Cora asked.

"Well, maybe banned is too strong," Porter said and chuckled. "Let's just say Gavin strongly encouraged me to leave investor relations to him."

Cora chortled, enjoying the time she was spending with him. It was a much easier conversation than the one she'd had with Drew or even Linus.

"Porter, man. What are you doing here?" Gavin said with a cheerful smile, approaching their table.

"Hey Gavin. Come and have a seat," Porter said. "You remember Cora?"

"Of course, Mystery Adventures, right?" Gavin asked. "So, do you like the Lunar Bakery as much as we do? We're here so much, this is our second home."

"The coffee is excellent, and so was the tea-cake," Cora said.

"The chocolate one?" Gavin asked.

Cora nodded.

"Had it last time," Gavin said. "It's my current favorite."

"On a different note, I'm looking into Aria Spencer's death," Cora said. "Do you mind if I ask you a few questions?"

Gavin stiffened and tried to cover it with a forced smile.

"No, of course not. Ask me whatever you want," Gavin said.

"Did you notice anything unusual before Aria passed?" Cora asked.

"No, not at all," Gavin said, relaxing his shoulders. "I got off the shuttle, and the first person I saw when I left the waiting area was

Porter." He selected a cup of coffee from the meal crafter. It materialized on the table with a lid a moment later. "Where was I? Oh, yes. Porter told me Drew and Jane were behind him and he wanted to avoid Drew. I started telling him about my meeting with our investors as I steered him away from Drew. But then I heard a lot of screaming."

"Uhmm... I may have forgotten the part about avoiding Drew," Porter said with a nervous laugh.

Cora examined him for a moment, wondering if she should chance lowering her shield.

"Did I say something wrong?" Gavin asked.

"No. It's my fault," Porter said in a low voice. He turned to Cora. "Do you have any more questions?"

"I looked at some vids from the spaceport," Cora said. "Gavin, you would've been facing Drew and Jane. Did anything strike you as odd before the screaming?"

"No," Gavin said, shaking his head. "But I have to admit, I focused more on our successful meeting." He turned to face Porter. "The reason I tracked you here is there's a problem at work, and I was wondering if I could get your help with it."

Cora raised her eyebrows at the suddenness of his comment. He hadn't appeared to be in a hurry when he first sat down. But she said nothing.

"Yeah, I've just finished my croissant," Porter said as he sprang to his feet and placed his cup, plate, and utensils into the recycling receptacle. "I can go with you now." He turned to Cora. "I'm sorry. Did you have any more questions?"

Cora shook her head.

"I'll finish my coffee, but you two don't have to wait," Cora said.

The two men stood and left the bakery. Cora gazed at their backs for a moment, wondering what had happened. What was she missing?

CHAPTER 12

"I didn't get a chance to talk to you last night," Cora said, sensing Brian's quiet contentment. She adjusted her fluffy pajamas while sitting at the dining table across from him. Hoping she wouldn't disturb his serenity, she launched into her question. "So, how's Hugo?"

"We set more parameters to help him decide if keeping me is a valuable addition to his plans," Brian said with a half-smile, straightening his brown business jumpsuit.

"You don't seem as panicked today as yesterday," she said with a quizzical expression.

"Somehow I feel everything will be alright," he said.

"Is this a case of you 'just knowing?'" she asked.

He nodded, but remained quiet.

"You know you make a lot of noise when you wake up early," she crossed her arms with a lopsided smile.

"No idea what you're talking about," he chuckled, selecting a slice of blueberry coffee cake.

She took a bite of a raspberry coffee cake on her plate.

"I've had an idea about Mystery Adventures," she said and took a sip of coffee. "I want to expand the landscape options to include lunar ones. Instead of having my players limited to Earth settings, they can now find treasures at the bottom of a crater or buried in a mountain—what? Why are you staring at me?"

"No reason," he said. "I like listening to you when you're excited about something. Keep going."

"Was I talking too long?" she asked as her face grew warm.

"Of course not." He chuckled. "You have a good idea. You already have fans here in Lunar City. Why not give them something they might like?"

She grinned, and her shoulders dropped. She hadn't doubted herself around Brian before.

"Will you also include a simulation about the different gravity effects?" he asked. "You know

Lunar City is at Earth gravity, but once you step outside, you're only at one-sixth of that gravity."

"I like that," she said, warming to the topic again. "I hadn't thought that through. Instead, I pondered how dangerous hiking on the surface could be because of the shifting stones."

"Yes, that's good," he said.

"Of course, I need to include lots of dust," she said with glee. "It'll make it more difficult to find hidden treasures."

Brian gazed at her with a soft smile.

"Okay, now you're really making me uncomfortable," she said, shifting in her seat. "What's going on?"

Brian reached across the table, and she offered her hand.

"I just realized how much I love you," he said, giving her a gentle squeeze. "You're the perfect woman for me."

Her mouth fell open with a gasp, and her mind grasped at the right words to say. Aunt Ferna stepped into the room before Cora could get anything out.

"Good morning, children," Aunt Ferna said. "Did you sleep well?" She bustled into the room and didn't seem to notice the difference in the atmosphere. Glancing at their breakfast plates, she wrinkled her nose. "Oh, I don't want that again."

"Did you sleep well last night?" Cora asked, doing her best to cover her tumbling emotions.

"No. I hardly slept last night," Aunt Ferna sighed and sank into a chair between Cora and Brian. "I let Kenna talk me into going to another casino. And you know I never drink, but last night I had a glass of lunar wine. Now I have a headache. Do you think there was something in that wine?"

Cora giggled at Aunt Ferna's comments.

"Maybe you're not used to the alcohol since you seldom ever drink." Cora said, patting Aunt Ferna's hand.

Brian stood and strode to his bedroom, and the door slid shut.

Cora felt his tumbling emotions and wished she could've said something before Aunt Ferna joined them.

"I only had one glass," Aunt Ferna said. She gazed at the shut door for a moment. "Is everything okay, dear? I noticed Brian didn't say much."

"Yes, everything's fine," Cora said. "I think he's worried about his business."

"Oh, yes. Benjamin's been telling me about that," Aunt Ferna said. "Those clients, they're terrible. I've been encouraging Benjamin to tell Brian to move back to Earth and restart his business. That way, he can support himself and he'll feel good."

Cora gazed at her aunt for a moment.

Did she know what Brian and I were talking about? she thought. *How does she always know what's going on?*

Her comm bracelet chimed, interrupting her thoughts. Jane appeared on a floating screen with rumpled hair and sleepy, puffy eyes.

"Morning," Jane said with a drawl, stifling a yawn.

"Good morning to you," Cora said. "What are you doing up so early?"

"There's something I want to talk to you about," Jane said with a wide yawn. "Sorry. Do you think you can meet me a little later today? Maybe we can have lunch together at my house?"

"Sure," Cora said. "Let me check with Brian to see if he can make it."

"You need his permission?" Jane snorted.

"I don't need his consent," Cora said with a frown. "He's helping with my investigation."

"Well, I don't care," Jane said. "Bring him or leave him."

The floating screen went dark. Cora closed it.

"Is that sweet little Jane?" Aunt Ferna asked, putting her teacup on the table. "I met her years ago when I first visited Lunar City. She and her sister were both darlings."

"I've spoken to her a few times now," Cora said with a huge sigh. "Many times she's... not nice, and I don't think Aria's passing is to blame."

"She's always pleasant when I meet her mom," Aunt Ferna said, taking another sip of tea.

Brian returned from his bedroom.

"Brian, Jane wants to meet around lunch," Cora said, forcing herself to lower her shoulders. She still sensed his repressed emotions and Aunt Ferna's interest. "Do you think you can make it?"

"I'll try," he said, pausing for a moment. "I can't guarantee it, though. Hugo and I still have a few things to work out."

"Yes, of course," Cora said. "I'll check with you again at noon. Have a good day."

Brian nodded and strode out of the room.

"I don't care what you say," Aunt Ferna said. "There's something bothering him."

She thought of all the replies she could have given Aunt Ferna, but all of them required a long explanation. And she didn't have it in her to start right now.

Cora strolled away from the Athos Tower and turned toward the Askov neighborhoods. She'd sent Brian a message, but he hadn't replied. During her walk, she gazed through the clear dome ceiling. But because of the new Earth phase, she only viewed a black circle surrounded by stars. It looked like an empty space in the sky and reminded her of the incomplete conversation she'd had with Brian. Should she have said 'I love you, too?' Did she love him?

After a fifteen-minute walk, she reached Jane's house. It was in the same neighborhood as Linus's, but it was at least one story taller. Like the other homes in the neighborhood, it resembled a gray, three-dimensional rectangle. She walked to the front door made of ornate carved faux wood.

"Coraline Brimble," the home's AI said. "Please wait a moment."

The front door swung inward, and Cora blinked in surprise. Most doors in Lunar City slid open. But she grinned as she ambled into the entryway and discovered another mini-forest with cool, moist air and the fresh scent of earth. It also put a delightful smile on her face like it did when she first entered the Rowleys' house. She followed the lights in the floor along a hallway to the back of the house, where she found a small sitting room. The room reminded her of something Aunt Ferna would like—a little old-fashioned but beautiful. Three sofas covered in floral prints dominated the space, which centered on a coffee table. There were images of flower paintings on three of the walls. A vid feed from Earth dominated the entire fourth wall, and it displayed a lush green forest complete with birds, chipmunks, and deer.

"Wow, where is that?" Cora asked with raised eyebrows. "It's gorgeous."

"Oh, some forest," Jane said with a dismissive wave of her hand. She sat on a sofa with its back to the entrance of the sitting room. "My mom told me, but I don't remember." She waved Cora closer. "Come and have a seat. Do you want some tea with a mid-morning snack?"

"No food, but I'd love some coffee," Cora replied, taking a seat on a sofa with Jane.

"Of course," Jane said, pressing a button on the coffee table. A moment later, a cup of hot coffee appeared in front of Cora in a sturdy mug. A cup of tea in a delicate floral cup appeared in front of Jane, accompanied by a floral print plate with four tiny cherry cakes.

They both took a sip of their drinks, and Jane took a bite of one of the tiny cherry cakes. When she finished chewing her cake, she turned to Cora.

Cora also lowered her shield by small increments. She sensed Jane's calm emotions and no one else in the house.

"So, what have you found so far?" Jane asked, wiping her mouth.

"Yes, let's get started with that," Cora said, taking one last sip of coffee. "Do you have Aria's death report?"

"Yeah, but only the preliminary," Jane said. "I'll send it to you right now." She pressed a button on her comm bracelet, sending the report.

A moment later, Cora's bracelet chimed. "Thanks," she said.

"I read through it, and I don't think you'll find it too useful," Jane said.

"I suspect you're right," Cora said. "The IPS doesn't seem too interested in doing a thorough investigation." She paused, gathering her thoughts. "Let's get started with what I found."

"Agent Taylor has interviewed you twice," Cora said. "They suspect you murdered your sister."

Jane nodded, but said nothing.

"What you didn't mention is that you're the only beneficiary of Aria's will," Cora said, sensing Jane's emotions. A wave of Jane's sadness washed over her and receded in slow, halting steps. "What I don't understand is why you hid that from me."

"How did you know about the will?" Jane asked and then held up both hands. "No, don't tell me it's your Aunt Ferna, isn't it?"

Cora shrugged her shoulders.

"I don't even blame your aunt," Jane said as exasperation spread over her face. "The problem is my mom, Linus's mom—actually, all our moms are chatterboxes. I'm sure your aunt had no problem finding out about the will."

"Well, I don't feel comfortable discussing what Aunt Ferna's been up to," Cora said, detecting Jane's mild amusement. "But I would like an answer to my question."

Jane sighed and stared down at the plate of tiny cakes.

"When Aria and I were little girls," Jane said in a low voice. "We were the best of friends, and we planned our lives together." She paused with a nostalgic look but continued staring at the plate. "We were both supposed to get married at the same time and have exactly two children. There were other things, but that doesn't matter now."

She paused and gazed at the vid for a moment while two chipmunks chased each other over several tree branches.

"Of course, our plans changed as we grew older," Jane continued. "One of the major changes was to each create a will and list the other as the beneficiary. The purpose was if one of us passed away, the other would be taken care of. If we had families, we'd change our wills to make our spouses the beneficiaries."

Jane shifted the tiny cakes on her plate, but she didn't eat.

"The reason is pretty straightforward," Jane said. "Even though we're Readers, we're not on the rich side of the Spencer family. That's Jessica, Mabel, and Alice. Jessica and Mabel never had children. Alice passed away, so her family inherited her shares of Spencer Industries, and they're rich. The problem is Jessica and Mabel both had a falling out with my father, who's their second cousin. So, Aria and I tried to secure our futures by ensuring our tiny mining shares would go to each other instead of back to Spencer Industries."

Jane took a sip of tea. Cora sensed she told the truth.

"Anyway, that was our plan," Jane said. "We told our parents about it, and they helped us do it. We made our wills when I turned eighteen, about five years ago."

"In your interviews with Agent Taylor," Cora said. "Did you discuss anything other than Aria's will and your Reader abilities?"

"No, she's useless," Jane scoffed. "I've given her so many other things to look into, but she's not interested."

"What have you talked to her about?" Cora asked.

"I told her it's strange that Aria and the entire Meadcroft family overslept that day," Jane said. "But Agent Taylor didn't care."

"I'll meet them in a couple of days," Cora said.

"Also, I mentioned Aria didn't talk to me with her mind that morning," Jane said. "She was a chatterbox, and I'd sometimes have to block her just so I could think. But when she woke up that morning, she hadn't sent a message... with her mind."

"You told me earlier she sent you a message about running late using your comm bracelet," Cora said.

"Yes, that was so unlike her, too," Jane said. "She almost never sent me information messages via our bracelets. When I presented these ideas to Agent Taylor, she dismissed them and mumbled something about wasting her time."

Jane gazed at the streaming vid, watching a deer picking its way along a trail. Cora sensed Jane's anger mixed with deep wells of sadness. Her emotions were not overwhelming yet, but Cora continued monitoring them all the same.

"I spoke to Linus and Porter," Cora said. "There's an unlikely coincidence that the five of you were at this spaceport at the time that Aria passed away. Something's going on. Something I can't see yet."

"What do you mean, five of us?" Jane asked.

"You, Aria, Linus, Drew and Porter," Cora said. "I mean, Gavin was there, but he's a recent friend."

"I've only met Gavin a few times," Jane said. "He's often with Porter."

"What I want to know is why you all dislike Linus?" Cora asked.

"Oh, that's a long story," Jane said with a sigh. "The short of it is, he's awful, and we got sick of him."

Suddenly, loud bangs interrupted their conversation. They seemed to come from the front door on the other side of the house.

Cora raised her shield in self-defense.

"Who's at the door?" Jane asked, addressing the home's AI.

"It's Drew Yarmouth," the home's AI replied.

"Well, let him in. Something must be wrong," Jane said, jumping to her feet and making her way to the sitting room's entrance.

Cora stood and followed.

They heard screaming and someone stomping down the hall toward them. A moment later, Drew burst into the room, shouting and gripping his head. With his eyes squeezed shut, he tripped over the sofa where they had been sitting and toppled onto the floor on the other side. Sandwiched between the sofa and the coffee table, he started writhing on the floor.

"It hurts! It hurts! Help me!" Drew screamed.

Cora and Jane raced to the coffee table, moving it away to make more room.

"Get the medipad," Cora yelled to Jane and then looked down at Drew. Her chest tightened. What should she do? "What's happening to you? How can we help you?"

Jane sprang to her feet and raced to the wall a few steps away from the sofa where she and Cora had been sitting. She pressed a tiny button, causing the medipad to pop out of the wall and float. Jane rushed it toward Drew.

Drew stopped moving with a final shudder and exhaled.

"He's gone," Cora said in a shaky voice. She lowered her shield for a moment, verifying she felt nothing and hurried to raise it again.

Jane reached Drew with the floating medipad. The probes from the medipad extended toward Drew. One attached to his head, and the other connected with his chest.

"Clear," a mechanical voice called from the medipad

Cora and Jane stepped away from the body and it spasmed as the medipad tried to resuscitate him. But Cora had seen this before, and he wasn't coming back. After a few more attempts, the medipad retrieved its probes, which disappeared by folding into its body. It remained floating and still.

"Drew Yarmouth is deceased," a mechanical voice called from the medipad. "Contacting Interplanetary Security."

Jane fell onto Drew's body with huge, wracking sobs.

"No, no," Jane cried. "You can't be gone now. Not you, too." She continued crying.

Cora held back tears. She hadn't much liked Drew, but she was very sorry for Jane.

CHAPTER 13

Fifteen minutes later, Agent Taylor paced into the house with four other agents behind her. She gave instructions to the other agents to scan for clues, secure the house, and locate Drew Yarmouth's parents.

Agent Taylor walked to the body and performed a preliminary scan.

"Verified. Drew Yarmouth is deceased," Agent Taylor said in a dry, detached voice. She instructed one of the agents to get a statement from Jane. Then she turned to Cora.

"Would you follow me?" Agent Taylor asked. "I want to get your statement in the next room."

Cora led the way out of the sitting room and through another door to a space that looked more like a formal living room. Gone were the soft florals, which were replaced by simple gray furniture and white walls adorned with black and white art. Cora took a seat on a gray hard-backed chair.

Agent Taylor remained standing and used her comm bracelet to make a private floating screen. She moved her fingers over the screen, preparing to take notes.

"Do you consent to being recorded?" Agent Taylor asked.

"Yes," Cora said, trying to calm herself and forget the image of Drew lying on the floor in the other room.

Concentrate, she thought. *I can't afford to let my guard down with the IPS.*

"Would you tell me what you were doing here?" Agent Taylor asked.

"I came to meet with Jane," Cora replied. "I promised her I would look into her sister Aria's death."

"Are you aware you're in violation of international law?" Agent Taylor asked with an edge in her voice. "The only people authorized to investigate crimes are members of the IPS or the EGS on Earth. Not a regular citizen like you."

Cora didn't reply but continued to control her emotions and concentrate on Agent Taylor's words.

If I reply, does that mean I'm admitting to a crime? Cora thought.

"Would you tell me in your own words what happened?" Agent Taylor asked, not pressing the issue.

"Yes," Cora began. "We heard banging on the front door."

She described the events of the afternoon and ended when Drew passed away.

"Do you think Jane was using her abilities to harm Drew?" Agent Taylor asked.

"No, of course not," Cora said. "We'd been talking before he entered. I went to school with many Readers. It takes quite a bit of concentration to do what you're implying—to actually put a suggestion in somebody's head and make them do something completely against their will. It's possible, but it takes a lot of focus and that's not what Jane was doing."

"Did you notice anything strange about Jane beforehand?" Agent Taylor asked. "Any unusual head motions? Any finger movements?"

"No," Cora said. "She wasn't doing anything to channel her abilities, if that's what you're asking. She was just having a conversation with me."

"What about your abilities?" Agent Taylor asked. "Weren't your sister and cousin able to control others as Feelers?"

"Yes, they were both very advanced Feelers," Cora said. "I was never that strong." She faltered at the last word as she remembered her final fight with her cousin. Winning that fight had cost her some self-respect. With enough concentration, she'd discovered she could force others to feel what she wanted. She shuddered.

"You don't have to be afraid," Agent Taylor smirked, misunderstanding Cora's reaction.

"I have an idea," Cora said. "Doesn't the IPS track the movement of Readers? Why not look at Drew's house and this one to see if a Reader's been by?"

"I already have a Reader in the next room," Agent Taylor said in a curt voice.

"You're wasting your time with Jane," Cora said.

"Why are you trying to defend Jane?" Agent Taylor asked. "Did she offer credits?"

Cora burst out laughing.

"That's the strangest thing I've heard from the IPS or the EGS," Cora said and continued chuckling.

Agent Taylor set her lips in a thin line.

"Jane. Jane," a voice in the hallway called. "Where are you?"

A moment later, an older couple rushed down the hall and past the open door where Cora sat.

"Jane's parents," Agent Taylor said, closing her floating window. She turned to Cora. "Stay here."

After a muffled conversation in the hall, Jane, her parents, and Agent Taylor returned to the modern sitting room.

Agent Taylor addressed Jane's parents and explained what had happened in their home.

Cora watched Jane sobbing again as her mom and dad joined her. She was grateful that she'd shielded herself earlier.

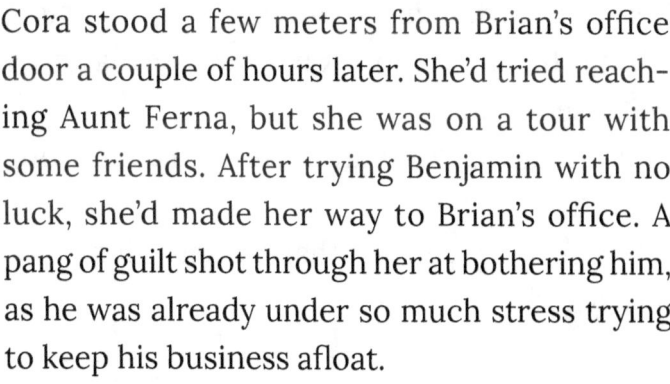

Cora stood a few meters from Brian's office door a couple of hours later. She'd tried reaching Aunt Ferna, but she was on a tour with some friends. After trying Benjamin with no luck, she'd made her way to Brian's office. A pang of guilt shot through her at bothering him, as he was already under so much stress trying to keep his business afloat.

She sighed, took a few steps, and peeked into Brian's office as the door slid open.

"Hey Brian," Cora said. "Are you busy?"

"I'm just wrapping things up," Brian said. "For once, I'm done at the end of a normal workday." He stood and walked around his desk to greet her. "Come in, come in." He guided her to a gray sofa next to the wall.

Something about her face must have alerted him.

"Something's happened," he said, grasping both of her hands. "Tell me everything."

Cora took a deep breath and shut her eyes, trying to fight off the image of Drew clutching his head. She opened them, gazing at Brian.

"Drew Yarmouth is dead," she said with a shudder. "I watched it happen right in front of me. He stormed into Jane's house, clutching his head and screaming something. 'Make it stop,' I think he said. And then a moment later he collapsed, dead."

Brian leaned closer and gave her a comforting hug.

"I'm so sorry you saw that," he said. "It sounds terrifying."

Cora shivered while he held her. When she stopped trembling, she pulled away, turning to face him.

"How are you feeling now?" he asked in a gentle voice.

"Scared, shaken," she said in a low voice. "I'm afraid if I continue the investigation. I might be next."

Brian opened and closed his mouth as if he wanted to reply but changed his mind.

"Who'd want to kill somebody that way?" she said. "It looked like a weapon designed to kill with maximum pain."

Brian gritted his teeth, holding back words.

"What I don't understand is what Drew was doing at Jane's house," Cora said. "Why didn't he use his comm bracelet and call the IPS or anybody else for help? Why her house?"

"Cora, this is exactly why I didn't want you to get involved in this investigation," Brian said, his lips set in a grim line. "There is a lunatic loose and bent on murdering people. For some reason, you've put yourself in his path. He's going to kill you in order to get to the other people on his list."

Cora didn't reply, but nodded. She withdrew her hands from Brian's and wrapped her arms around her torso.

"Look Cora," he said in a gentler voice. "I know you want to be helpful, but this is very dangerous. I think you should stop and let the IPS do its job."

"But I think I'm finally making some progress with Jane," she said. "There are some things—"

"No, Cora," he said, folding his arms and glaring at her. "I don't want to hear about it. The only thing I want to hear from you is that you have stopped the investigation."

Cora blinked a few times. Brian had never spoken to her like that.

"I'm sorry, but I just can't let it go," she said with a heavy sigh. "I have this feeling inside of me that if I ignore this, a lot more people are going to die. It's true—I might be one of them. But if one more person dies, and it was because I sat around and did nothing, I wouldn't be able to live with myself."

Brian huffed and shot to his feet. He stalked around his desk and ended up at their sofa, but he didn't take his seat again.

"Cora, I love you," he said. "I want to spend the rest of my life with you. But I can't stand by while you put yourself in danger. It doesn't make any sense."

"It makes sense to me," she said in a low voice. "If you thought about it for a while, it'd make sense to you, too." She sighed and climbed to her feet. "Last year, you gave up your job at Albright Corp because you have a strong sense of right and wrong. You were actually trying to save your family's business. But your mom and sister weren't able to see that. You were in the right, and I supported you. Why can't you support me now?"

"This is completely different," he said in a raised voice. "Whether my family's business thrives or goes under, nobody's going to die. But if you find the murderer or not, you could still die. There's no comparison between our two cases."

"We're the same, Brian," she said. "Neither of us can let an injustice slide when we could do something about it."

Taking large strides to his desk, he plopped onto his chair and crossed his arms.

"I'm sorry," Cora said with a frown. "I shouldn't have come here when I was so upset." She turned to leave.

"No wait," Brian said, standing and stepping toward her. He enveloped her in a warm embrace. "Look, I understand you're shaken up. I don't want you to be alone. Let me close everything here and we'll walk back to our suite."

She nodded and waited a moment as he closed several floating screens over his desk. They exited his office.

It's strange the thing that makes us so similar is also the thing that makes us incompatible, she thought.

———————— ✑ ————————

The following day, in her suite, Cora leaned back on her sofa with her head buried among two floating screens. She was avoiding thinking about the fight she'd had with Brian. Working her way through the Net, she looked for information about Aria, Drew, Jane, Linus, and Porter.

She dove into Arias' past and discovered nothing unusual. Aria had become a music composer and also taught a few students. But she only worked with other Askovs.

Next, she examined the information she discovered about Drew. Few things happened to him. She discovered he'd graduated, but she couldn't find any evidence of a career. Finding a small mention of a clipper accident, she followed the trail.

The accident turned out to be a huge accident. Three people died—a mother and two children. As she dug further, she gasped when she realized Drew, Linus, Porter, and Jane had been racing over an affluent Originals homesteading section just outside of Lunar City. Linus had crashed into the Varney's family home. Linus had ejected at the last minute and was unharmed.

As Cora's research continued, she found the IPS had tried to cover up the accident, but the Originals became irate and petitioned the government. Lunar City didn't have a traditional government. Instead, a group of elders sat on the council and made political decisions for the city.

With time, the Originals' pressure had resulted in Linus being brought to trial. Even though the evidence showed his guilt, he received only five years' probation because the judge had deemed it an accident. Cora tried looking for more information about the family. They were Originals and the only family member left alive was the dad, Xavier Varney, who was at work when it had happened.

The wife and children were well known and liked in the Originals' community, and that was the source of the huge outcry before and after the trial. In any case, he and a few cousins had moved to Earth a few weeks after the trial. She found family images of Xavier, his wife, and two children. The entire family was fit, the result of working on their homestead. Xavier had white-blond hair with pale blue eyes, while his wife and kids had light brown hair and blue-gray eyes.

A frisson of excitement raced down her back. Maybe she'd found the motive for the murders. But why those five people at the spaceport? Aria wasn't racing that day—why kill Aria?

Did Aria ever race with them? Cora thought.

Suddenly, the door to the suite slid open. Startled, Cora straightened on the sofa and gazed at Steven strolling through the door.

"Ugh… Do you ever knock?" Cora grumbled. "This is a private space."

"I know, and I'm sorry about that," Steven said, not looking even a bit sorry. "I needed to talk to you about Drew Yarmouth's murder."

Cora tried to sense his emotions, but detected nothing. She closed her floating screens.

"Tell me," Cora said.

"Agent Taylor is very close to arresting Jane," he said. "She only needs to convince her bosses to go along with her evidence."

"Yeah, she interviewed me yesterday." She shuddered as Drew's image popped into her mind's eye.

"By the way, she also suspects you," he said as he stood and started pacing around the sofa.

"I got that from the way she interviewed me," she said with a smirk. "I've dealt with incompetent EGS agents before. The IPS couldn't be too much worse."

"Looking at vids of the twenty-four hours before Drew died, I can't find anything," he said. "There was no point when something unusual happened. I can't figure out how the murderer got to him, and that scares me. I found the same thing when I looked at the twenty-four hours before Aria's death, too."

Steven plopped onto the sofa next to Cora with a huff.

"Would you mind if I had a cup of coffee?" he asked. Cora leaned over the coffee table, pressed a button and two cups of coffee materialized in front of them. They each took a sip, and Steven exhaled.

"I'm stuck," he said. "I can't figure out what the murderer did. It must be something high tech, but I can't figure out what that was. I don't even have a direction to start."

"Well, I can't figure out the tech, but I discovered something interesting," she said. She continued explaining how odd it was that all five people were in the spaceport at the same time, even though they had been there for different reasons. Four of them are involved in an accident that killed the Varney family five years ago. It's the same year Aria and Jane created their wills. I think this is all related.

"That sounds like a viable theory," he said, furrowing his eyebrows. "I can look into the Varneys' life here in Lunar City."

"I'll use my contacts in Tymal," she said. "They lived in a residential area outside of Lunar City—they were wealthy. I think they'd stay close to a prosperous city."

"Now, I have something to do," Steven said with a grim smile.

"The only slight issue is Aria wasn't racing," she said. "I can't figure out why someone would kill her."

"She was dating Drew," he said. "Maybe she helped him in some way."

"Good point," she said, warming her hands on her coffee cup. "Also, the day Aria passed away, she overslept."

"She was so perfect she never overslept," he scoffed.

"You interrupted me," she glared. "She was supposed to meet Jane and Drew at home. Instead, she sent them a message by her comm bracelet, asking them to meet her at the airport."

"Sounds normal to me," he smirked.

"She was a *Reader*," she said. "Used to being in touch with her sister several times a day. Why would she use her comm bracelet?"

"Oh..." he replied. "Did she oversleep or was it everyone in the house?"

"Now you understand," she said. "Everyone in the house."

"But I looked at the night vids," he said. "No one entered or left their home."

"I'm sure you're right," she said with a sigh. "The home's AI would have never admitted a stranger."

"I'll take a second look at the vids anyway," Steven said. "Maybe I missed something."

"Also, we should look into any sort of criminal links," Cora said. "I can't imagine it with Aria, but maybe with Drew or Linus. Porter also seems squeaky clean, but it wouldn't hurt to check him out."

"I can do that with my links to the casino bosses," he said.

"I hope you're not still gambling," she said in a scolding tone.

"Not as regularly as I used to. Don't worry." He stood, gulped the rest of his coffee, and paced around the sofa again.

Cora considered reminding him of how her cousin had controlled him by using his debts against him. But not wanting to start a painful conversation, she left it alone.

"Since I have ties to that world, I should be able to find something," he said. "But casino owners don't 'take care of' people so publicly," he added using air quotes. "They need customers to continue coming to their casinos and can't afford the negative publicity. Usually, the

Net reports an unexplained dead body in the middle of the night."

"I see what you mean," she said. "It's as if the killer meant for everyone to view these deaths. I wonder if the killer intended for Drew to perish in a public place. I assumed he was home and ran to Jane's house. Maybe Drew was supposed to die on a walkway."

"Well... take a look at this," he said, using his comm bracelet to bring up a floating screen.

Cora watched its contents, and it showed Drew in Central Park, sitting by the little pond. He levitated a rock and placed it in an artistic pattern with other rocks. Suddenly, he rubbed his head and lurched forward. His face contorted into pure terror as he leaped to his feet and began running.

"He ran straight to Jane's house," he said as he paused the vid. "But I don't know why he didn't ask for help in the park."

"I didn't see anyone else in your vid," she said. "This seems as if the killer intended Drew to die in the park—a public setting. It also means the killer knew Drew. Otherwise, how would he know to strike in the middle of the day with so few people around?"

"So, we'll both look into the Varney family," Steven said. "And you'll talk to the Meadcroft girl."

"Let me know if you need help with the casino owners," Cora said. "I feel like we finally have a new direction to investigate."

CHAPTER 14

Cora sat at the dining room table by herself in her mauve pajamas, a couple of days later. Without having to check his bedroom, Cora sensed Brian had left earlier. But Aunt Ferna and Benjamin were home.

Sitting at the table, waves of sadness rolled over her. She thought about the fight she'd had with Brian the previous evening, and how it looked like their relationship would never work.

Caught in with her thoughts, she missed Aunt Ferna entering the common area. She actually jumped when Aunt Ferna put a comforting hand over hers.

"My dear, what's wrong?" Aunt Ferna asked in a gentle voice, wearing a fluffy blue robe. "Have you and Brian had a tiff?"

"How do you always know what's going on?" Cora said, with a half-smile.

"I don't know," Aunt Ferna said with a shrug. "It's always been that way. And it helped me, a few times, get away from your mom." Cora's mom had bullied Aunt Ferna because she had no special abilities. Also, their parents never protected her aunt.

"Well, if she was anything like my sister, I don't envy you," Cora said.

"Now, tell me all about it," Aunt Ferna said. "What's happening between you two? Does this have to do with Drew?"

Cora explained she had seen Drew's death, and now Brian wanted her to stop the investigation. She felt the killer was going to murder someone else. And she couldn't sit by and let other people die.

Aunt Ferna nodded and patted her hand.

"When did you have this conversation?" Aunt Ferna asked.

"Right after Agent Taylor finished with me," Cora said. "I went to see him at his office and we were both upset."

"Of course, dear," Aunt Ferna said. "Unfortunately, that was not the right time to have that conversation. I'm sure you were upset after seeing somebody die." She wrinkled her eyebrows. "By the way, why didn't you message me?"

"I tried," Cora said with a sigh. "You were busy."

"Well, never mind about that," Aunt Ferna said. "I think the real remedy here is to give both of you time to sort through your feelings. You've had a terrible shock. And he's not happy that his beloved is in danger." She tutted. "It's a complicated mess, and only cool heads can work through this."

"What's going on?" Benjamin said, strolling into the room in his pajamas.

"The lovebirds have had a little tiff," Aunt Ferna said.

"Aunt!" Cora said in an exasperated voice.

"Well, it's true," Aunt Ferna said.

"Not quite," Cora said. "We have a complete difference in values. I don't see how we can fix this."

"Does this have to do with the death of that poor boy?" Benjamin asked. "Drew, was it?"

"Yes," Cora said, nodding. "Drew Yarmouth. I was visiting Jane when he ran in, clutching his head and screaming. Then, he collapsed to the floor dead, just like Aria."

"Sounds dreadful," Benjamin said with a shiver. "So naturally, you spoke to Brian, and he ordered you to stop the investigation," he said with a dry chuckle.

"That's the gist of it," Cora said.

"I still think if you wait a few days, or maybe a week, you'll come up with a solution," Aunt Ferna said.

"You know Ferna has a good point," Benjamin said. "There's probably a happy middle ground here. You only have to work together."

"The problem is Brian's planning to go to Mars," Cora said. "It helps his business. So, we don't have that much time before he leaves."

"Well," Benjamin said with a half-smile. "That shortens the time frame a bit. He could come in a later star cruiser. But the entire trip takes about eight months. So, he'd be by himself. That's a long time to be isolated amongst some strangers."

"My dear, is there something we can do?" Aunt Ferna asked.

"I don't think so," Cora said. "Maybe you're right, and I need to give things more time."

Cora left the suite, heading for the Meadcrofts' house. She strolled through winding walkways full of rectangular block homes. Occasionally, she passed a cluster of trees and synthetic plants, which disrupted the endless rows of gray houses. The neighborhood still brought down her mood, though. The Meadcroft family lived in the affluent Askov neighborhood area, close to the Spencer's home.

She thought about Brian and how she could fix things with him. Her mind kept going back to the moment he'd said he loved her, and she wondered what she should have done differently. What could she have said? Of course, then she also remembered Aunt Ferna had interrupted them.

After several minutes, she stood in front of the Meadcrofts' home. She took in the dull, gray view before walking to the front door.

"Good morning, Coraline. Brimble," the home's AI greeted her in a cheery voice.

Cora raised an eyebrow—most people didn't add a personality mod to their home's AI. After a few days of dealing with perpetual cheeriness, it usually got on your nerves.

"Hello," Cora replied.

"Wait a moment while I verify your appointment," the AI said, pausing for several seconds. "Please enter and follow the lights in the floor to the living room. You will meet with Ethel Meadcroft first." The door slid open.

"Oh..." Cora said, not expecting to meet Ethel. She knew Ethel from her quarterly meetings at the Albright Corp. She was soft-spoken but firm, especially during negotiations.

Cora took a few steps inside and gazed around the entry. She'd expected a mini-forest and cool, moist air like the other homes. Instead, cold gray walls greeted her. Her shoulders drooped.

She took a moment to lower her shield in small increments. She sensed three people in the house, and they were all calm.

Following the lighting, she paced toward the center of the house and turned right. Then her face lit up with a bright smile.

"I see," Cora said. "You put the forest in the living room. This is lovely."

"I know you were expecting something like the Spencer home," Ethel said, standing and pacing toward Cora with a small smile. She was an older woman with wavy gray hair and intelligent blue eyes. They shook hands and ambled to a comfortable, soft, faux leather sofa.

"Wilma's running late," Ethel said. "But she'll be here shortly. Would you like some tea or muffins?"

Cora felt Ethel's calm efficiency and thought she might need that if Wilma became upset.

"Well, maybe a cup of coffee," Cora said.

Ethel pressed a button on the coffee table in front of the sofa and two cups of coffee materialized in front of each woman.

"I needed to speak to you before you talked to Wilma," Ethel said. "Wilma is still very upset about losing Aria. They were inseparable for most of their lives, and I'd say she's not exactly herself now. I understand you're trying to find out who did this to Aria, but if you could please be gentle with Wilma, I'd appreciate it."

"Of course, I know this must be hard for her," Cora said. "I only have a handful of questions for her." She took a sip of coffee.

"I can't understand why anybody would want to harm Aria," Ethel said with a frown. "She was the kindest soul."

"That's the impression I've gotten based on her family and friends I've spoken to," Cora said.

A shuffle of footsteps interrupted their conversation. A woman in her mid-twenties with wavy black hair entered. She had her mom's bright blue eyes, but her face was pale and sickly.

Cora sensed deep wells of never-ending sadness—her heart ached for Wilma.

"Sorry I'm late," Wilma said in a quiet voice. She shuffled into the room, taking the plush chair opposite the sofa. She folded her feet under her and sat on them.

"It's quite alright," Cora said with a gentle smile. "I've enjoyed talking to your mom. I'll try not to take up too much of your time."

"So, what would you like to know?" Wilma asked.

"Did you notice anything unusual in your house the night before Aria passed away?" Cora asked.

"No, nothing at all," Wilma said, shaking her head. "It was a typical night. I was happy to see Aria before she went on vacation." Her despair spiked when she mentioned Aria.

Cora thought she might need to raise her shield, but waited instead. She also sensed some anxiety from Ethel.

"We stayed in my room most of the time," Wilma said. "But at dinnertime, we both came out and ate in the dining room. Mom joined us and so did my brother, but not Dad."

"My husband's running for re-election," Ethel said. "He's been working a lot of late hours."

"I just want to clarify. The only people at home were your mom and brother?" Cora said.

"Yes," Wilma said.

"No," Ethel said. "My husband returned very late. Everybody had gone to bed. I don't really know what time that was."

"Okay. Thanks for clearing that up," Cora said and turned back to Wilma. "The following morning, after you woke. Did you notice anything odd?"

"Yes," Wilma said, her eyebrows furrowed. "Aria seemed scattered. I wasn't sure what to make of that. She's normally very organized and in control. But that morning, she couldn't find her things. They weren't in the right spot. She was flustered. A few times, she struggled to even come up with words to describe what she was looking for. It was very unlike her."

"Did she continue like that the entire morning?" Cora asked.

"Yeah," Wilma said. "Also, she couldn't reach her sister with her mind. So, she had to send a comm message. Eventually, she got everything ready and raced out of the house. I didn't realize I wouldn't see her again."

Fresh waves of Wilma's sadness washed over Cora, and this time she raised her shield.

"Since Aria passed away, has anything strange happened in your house?" Cora asked.

"No," Wilma said with a frown. "What do you mean by strange?"

"Anything that should've happened but didn't?" Cora said. "Or maybe something that did happen, but seems unimportant?"

"No," Wilma said with a sigh. "Everything's been fine."

"How often do you look at the logs of who enters and exits your home?" Cora asked. She thought of how someone could enter the home without the AI catching them.

"Uhmm... never," Ethel said.

"Can you ask your home's AI what time your husband came home?" Cora asked.

"Oh, sure," Ethel said. She raised her voice. "What time did Norman come home the night Aria spent the night?"

"Norman Meadcroft entered the home at eleven forty-seven in the evening," the AI replied.

"That sounds right," Ethel said. "I thought it was very late. We would've been asleep."

"Very well. Thank you so much for your time," Cora said. "Please let me know if you think of something else that might help me discover what happened to Aria."

"Of course," Wilma said.

Cora stood, nodded to Wilma, and turned to leave. Ethel followed her out of the room and down the hallway. They stopped at the front door.

"Thank you so much for being gentle with Wilma," Ethel said.

"I truly hope she feels better soon," Cora said, turning to step outside.

Wilma confirmed everything Jane said, Cora thought. *But I'm still missing something.*

CHAPTER 15

Around noon the next day, Cora left her suite and ambled past Central Park along the edge where it met the Askov neighborhood. She planned to meet Porter and take the flying train, also called the Flyer. After a few minutes, she found the waiting area where a group of eleven people waited with her. They wore colorful clothing and didn't have a Lunar City drawl. Tourists, she guessed.

"Hello," Porter said, a little out of breath. "I thought I wasn't going to make it. Gavin found a problem with our code, but I decided Aria was more important."

"I'm glad you're helping me," Cora said and glanced at the growing crowd. "I'm looking forward to taking the Flyer. I've never taken a flying train." She grinned, a little giddy.

"The Flyer is Lunar City's only airborne train. " Porter said. "All other trains run on antigrav tracks like LARA in Tymal."

"Also the Flyer lets me see Lunar City's landmarks from several meters in the air," Cora said.

Porter burst out laughing.

"I've never heard it put that way," Porter said, continuing to chuckle. "The city's not old enough to have landmarks."

A few minutes later, the train came to rest in front of the crowd that had swelled to about twenty-five people. Fifty or so people stepped off the train, while she and Porter surged in and scrambled for a seat. Cora grabbed the window seat, and Porter sat next to her.

Cora gazed at the train's narrow walkway with two seats on each side. The very basic blue seats all faced the same way but had ample leg room. She glanced at the gray floor, walls, and ceiling. They only differed by shades of gray with the lightest on the ceiling. She turned to gaze through the window. After everybody boarded, the doors closed.

"Please remain seated," the train's AI said in a dry mechanical voice. "Do not stand at any point throughout the train's ascent, flight, and descent. Anyone violating these rules will be belted in their seats." Cora wondered how they were going to force somebody, who was already out of their seat, into a seat belt, but left it alone.

The Flyer ascended into the air with a gentle lift and easy mid-air turns. Cora giggled, exhilarated. After a moment, a tiny whooshing sound erupted from the back of the train and it began drifting forward. It executed a second graceful turn as it headed back toward the park. It felt nothing like a hovercar, which maneuvered through the air with sharp turns.

"Why did you want to meet in the Originals Dome?" Cora asked.

"I wanted you to see the less glamorous side of Lunar City," Porter said in a schoolteacher tone. "Many Askovs, born and raised here, have never visited this dome."

"Why? Are they afraid?" Cora asked.

"No. They feel it's not worth their time to learn about Originals," Porter said with a sigh. "This leads the Askovs to enact all sorts of injustices."

Cora paused for a moment, wishing she could lower her shield and sense his emotions.

"Is there something specific you want me to learn?" she asked.

"Not really," he said. "Only the general sense that they're humans deserving of respect."

"And you think I'm not capable of understanding they're people?" Cora asked with a smirk. "Maybe you're the only Askov capable of understanding them?"

Porter shifted in his seat, cleared his throat, and turned to the front of the train.

Cora gazed through the window at the tourist area where she'd been staying as the Flyer glided past. It drifted over Central Park where she'd gone for a walk with Brian just a few days ago. And the thought of Brian made her heart hurt again. But she shook her head and focused on her adventure. The train floated over the business section, which looked similar to the Askov residential section, except with taller buildings that contained a lot more glass.

Porter remained quiet, and Cora, wanting to fill the silence, started their conversation again.

"Looks like we're going into a tunnel," she said.

"It connects the Lunar City main dome with the Originals Dome," he said with relief in his voice.

After five minutes, the Flyer emerged into the new dome. It looked quite different from the main dome, because every building had been positioned in random places with lots of spidery walkways connecting them. Also, each building was a shade of gray or tan and only reached one or two stories.

"There aren't any parks," she said, a little disappointed. "Just a wide street through the middle of the dome hemmed with stores."

"That's Main Street," he said. "It has three blocks of small shops for specialty foods, bakeries, and, of course, coffee."

Drifting to one end of Main Street, the train made its way to the waiting area. The other end of Main Street split into several walkways that led to the spidery network of paths linking to each home.

The Flyer lowered out of the sky with gentle turns and came to rest at the waiting area. Cora and Porter filed out with the rest of the passengers.

"This looks like downtown Tymal," she grinned, peering at the grassy center street lined on both sides by rows of small stores. The bustle of the shoppers criss-crossing to get to the next store made her feel at home. "Where are the hovercars?"

"They're not allowed inside the dome," he said. "Safety reasons. Let's walk this way." He gestured toward one side of the street.

"Hovercars are banned?" she asked. "But we're walking along a street."

"Originally, everyone had access to hover-cars, but after a nearly fatal accident, the council moved to ban them," he said.

They ambled past a place that sold vegetables grown in the moon's soil. But the aromas from the bakery made her stop and peer in.

"Come on, I have more to show you," he said with a chuckle.

They strolled past a coffee shop and several tourist knick-knack stores. As they passed a row of restaurants, Cora stopped at one that specialized in crystallized lunar vegan food.

"I love crystallized vegetables," Cora said.

"They have good food," Porter said. "But I think you'll really like our destination."

She pulled herself away, and they continued winding their way among tourists until the end of the street. They crossed at the end of the street and walked two doors back in the direction they'd come.

"Another coffee shop?" she asked. "Why didn't we stop at the six or so we already passed?"

"This is the Martian Coffee shop," he said with a chuckle. "The coffee's okay, but the pastries are fantastic."

"Why are there so many Martian stores in Lunar City?" Cora asked, stepping through the front door.

"Everything Martian is fashionable," he said. "It's been that way for a few years, but something else will take its place soon."

Cora smirked.

They took their seats at a nearby table.

"What do you recommend here?" she asked.

"The Martian sprout sandwich," he said.

She wrinkled her nose, and Porter chuckled.

"It's not as bad as it seems," he said.

"Do you have anything a little more filling?" she asked. "Lasagna? Chicken?"

"Yes, they have the best Martian Chicken salad," he said.

"Now, hold on," Cora said with a half-smile. "How can you make chicken Martian?"

"Well, they call it that," Porter said. "But they're really referring to the bed of crystallized vegetables it's served on."

"Perfect," Cora said as she scrolled through the menu on the meal crafter and made her selection.

"I've already eaten," Porter said. "So, I'm going to have dessert." He scrolled through the menu and ordered a raspberry puff pastry and a coffee.

A moment later, the food materialized onto their table.

"Either the chicken salad is excellent or I'm hungry," she said, taking another bite.

"It's probably the best in Lunar City," he said, taking a sip of coffee. "The pastry is good, too."

"I'm curious. Would you tell me about your business?" she asked. "I think I heard you owed credits to Drew. What happened?"

"It's a long story," he said with a sigh. "I'm a little embarrassed."

"I'd really like to know," she said.

"Okay," he said, nodding his head. "I launched my company three years ago, and everything was going great. I had enough credits to pay everybody, but no reserves for emergencies. Then we hit a snag where some of the code stopped working. The AI, Gavin, and I worked for three days without sleep trying to debug it. We also lost more than half our customers, but we couldn't find the problem. We needed a more advanced AI, but that required credits." He stopped to take a sip of coffee.

"What did you do?" she asked in a quiet voice.

"I borrowed credits from Drew, Linus, and Gavin. I thought once I purchased the advanced AI and got my users back, I'd earn credits again and pay them back. It didn't work out that way. We got the advanced AI, and it fixed the problems, but the users didn't come back right away. It took one and a half years. Everyone was fine with waiting until I could repay them. Our customer base was growing."

"What was the problem?" she asked.

"A virus," he scowled. "It was something so advanced we couldn't remove it. We lost several months of work and had to go back to a previous copy. But at least the new AI is better at checking our new code for viruses."

"So, what happened with Drew?" she asked.

"At first, no one cared much about the amount of time I took to pay them back," he said. "Then Drew got into trouble for cheating. Aria's family threatened to break their engagement. It was a mess. They reached some sort of settlement, resulting in Drew breaking it off with Trudy and paying additional credits to Aria's family. He needed the credits right away so he could get married. This led to a lot of fights between me and Drew. I tried to apologize, but his family put a lot of pressure on him. Things got worse the longer it took to regain our customers."

"What happened to Trudy?" she asked.

"Drew dropped Trudy and humiliated her," he said with an edge to his voice. "Originals are less understanding than Askovs about affairs outside of an agreement. Drew needed more credits to appease Aria's family, but Trudy's family turned on her. I helped her purchase a ticket so she could move to Earth. She has aunts and uncles that are taking care of her now. I was forced to be civil with Drew because I had to repay him, but I hated what he did to Trudy."

Cora couldn't help it and lowered her shield for a moment before raising it again. She sensed his intense wave of hatred that faded to sadness.

"I know that sounds bad," he said in a quiet voice. "But I didn't kill him."

"How did you know Trudy?" she asked.

"She's a sister to one of my coworkers," he said. "I introduced her to Drew." He shook his head. "I didn't approve of their behavior, but she didn't deserve to be fired from her job and ostracized by her family."

"You realize this gives you a strong motive," she said. "Has the IPS questioned you?"

"No, and I prefer to keep it that way," he frowned. "My business is running fine now, but we still don't have enough to weather a major setback."

Cora paused, examining him while he sipped his coffee with trembling hands.

"I want to understand your funding a little more," she asked. "When Drew and Linus loaned you credits, they would've used their family ties, right?"

Porter nodded, downing the last of his coffee.

"Where did Gavin get that many credits?" Cora asked.

"Don't know," Porter said, selecting a second cup of coffee from the meal crafter. "Some Originals have generational wealth, but Gavin never talks about his family."

"He seems protective of you," Cora said.

"He's been like a father figure to me," he said with a wry smile. "I mean, he's only ten years older than me, but he's... wise. He's helped me out so many times just by giving me advice. Also, I would've never been able to find the virus in our software without him. I almost lost my business."

"Was Gavin born here?" she asked.

"No, he was born in Tymal," he said, taking a sip from a fresh cup of coffee. "The Smith family is there—a couple of cousins, I think."

"How did you hire him?" she asked.

"He came recommended," he said, scrunching his eyebrows. "One of the Meadcroft brothers." He chuckled. "Also, I hired a lot of young programmers, and sometimes they're... not professional. But Gavin manages them with subtle requests, keeping them in line. Things run better when he's around."

Cora glanced around the cafe, thinking, but she noticed several people glaring at her. Since she'd been shielded, she hadn't noticed their attention at first.

"What's happening?" she asked in a lowered voice. "Are they angry? Frightened?"

"Oh, that..." he said, turning to meet everyone's eyes. "You're a new element here, and the Originals aren't used to you. They're mostly afraid you're going to hurt one of them. If you live here longer, they'll get used to you, eventually."

"But I'm a Feeler. I sense others' emotions," she said, frowning.

"Feelers are able to control and manipulate others, too," he said, raising one eyebrow. "They have a right to be afraid."

"Having an ability doesn't automatically make you bad," Cora said, pursing her lips.

"It did in my family," Porter said, his eyes boring into hers. "There's a reason I live in Lunar City while the rest of my family is in Tymal."

"Your family are Listeners, but you have no abilities," she said. "Does that mean a sibling bullied you?"

He took a sip of coffee and didn't reply.

Cora reflected on the power dynamic between herself and her sister and also between her mom and Aunt Ferna.

He has a point about those with power abusing it, but it's a narrow way of thinking, Cora thought.

"So, you've been in Lunar City for years," she said. "The Originals must approve of you."

"It's more that they know I'm just like them," he said with a little pride in his voice. "I come from an Askov family, but not the rich branch. Also, they disowned me when I turned eighteen."

"Should I ask about that?" she asked in a somber tone.

"No," Porter said, rising to his feet. "I think we need to make our way back to the Flyer."

Cora glanced at the neighboring tables and they quickly looked away as she met their eyes. She couldn't sense their emotions, but their behavior made her uneasy. If she hadn't been there with Porter, she had a feeling she would not be welcome.

"I think you're right," Cora said, standing and following Porter out the door.

After Cora stepped off the Flyer, she found herself wandering through Central Park. She meandered over various trails, feeling rejuvenated by all the lush green trees and plants surrounding her. The occasional child raced past her with glee in their eyes, but their happiness didn't touch her. Before she knew it, she was standing at the edge of the park and gazing across the busy walkway surrounding it. On the other side was the Business Center where Brian's office was located.

She shifted from foot-to-foot for a moment before stepping onto the walkway, dodging passersby, and entering one of the tall business buildings. Taking the antigrav lift to the seventeenth floor, she stepped out and stood on a taupe carpet. She turned to the left and gazed at Brian's office door. Lowering her shield for a moment, she sensed his rolling emotions as he struggled to hold them in check.

She raised her shield again, took a deep breath, and strolled to the door. It slid open.

"Hello," Cora said with a small smile.

Brian's head shot up, and he stared at her, confused for a moment. Then his face hardened.

"What are you doing here?" Brian asked, his face arranged into a stiff, angry mask.

She remained at the door, shifting foot-to-foot

"I haven't seen you for a couple of days," she said with a shrug, but she remained at the door. "I wanted to say hello."

Brian took a deep breath and stared down at his desk. His shoulders lowered a little.

"Is there something you want?" he said in a kinder tone.

"No. Not sure," she said. She didn't need her abilities to detect his emotions now.

"Look, Cora," he said, his lips set and a grim line. "I love you. But I need time to think about what I want from our relationship. And I think you need time, too."

"Yeah, you're right," she said, nodding. "I'll see you later at the suite."

"Not sure I'll be there anytime soon," he said. "There's a lot going on now."

She turned and strolled away.

Lowering her shield again, she felt his waves of sadness. But if she tried to go back, she knew he'd use his defenses and become angry again.

Feeling defeated, she wracked her brain for a solution to their problem while she made her way back to their suite.

CHAPTER 16

Cora's eyes popped open, and she stared at the ceiling, disoriented. She'd been dreaming she was reading in her Tymal bedroom, and it took her several seconds to recognize the constant chime from her comm bracelet. After she realized she was in Lunar City, she rolled over and squinted at her chiming bracelet. She answered the vidchat and an image of Steven Marsh appeared on the screen.

"What do you want?" Cora said in a creaky voice. "It's the middle of the night."

"Quiet! This is urgent," Steven said with a pinched face. "Throw on your clothes while I explain."

"This is ridiculous!" Cora said in a raised voice.

"Someone has broken into Jane's house," Steven said with panic etched on his face. "I need you to go there and stop him."

Cora snickered.

His image flickered, replaced by a figure dressed in black from head to toe. He stepped through their living room and down the hall in slow, methodical steps.

"Oh..." Cora said, springing off the bed. "Call IPS."

"I did," Steven said. "There's some sort of war going on in the Casino Dome. Every IPS agent is busy. Please get dressed and help Jane."

Cora raced to her closet, peeled off her pajamas, and threw on a long-sleeved top and mismatched pants.

"I'll go to her house, but I don't have the skills to stop someone like that," Cora said, slipping into her boots.

"I'm sending Linus; he's armed," Steven said. "I need you there in case whatever that is becomes invisible." He turned to something off-screen. "Keep this screen open."

"Becomes invisible? What's going on?" Cora said, sprinting out the door of her suite, hesitating at the entrance to the stairs.

"Skip the stairs," Steven said in a frenzied tone. "The lift will be faster. I've fixed it."

When she reached the ground floor, she stepped out of the antigrav lift into the lobby and sprinted out of the door into the darkness. The filters over the dome darkened to simulate nighttime, but she followed the subtle lighting inside the walkways that allowed her to see. She loped through winding walkways toward the Askov neighborhood.

"I may have figured out what that military thing does, but I'm not sure," Steven said. "I found some specs and it hints the thing could turn invisible to our sensors and even to humans."

After a few turns, she stood in front of the Spencer's home.

"How do I get in?" Cora asked, turning to Steven displayed on the floating screen.

"Wait for me!" Linus yelled, racing to the front door in what looked like tan pajamas and holding a blaster.

"I've opened the door," Steven said. "Just run through, go up the stairs, and get to the second door on the left."

"Let me go first," Linus said, stepping forward.

"He's entered her bedroom." Steven said in a pinched voice. "Hurry!"

Cora raced forward behind Linus. They found the stairs and took them two at a time. As she reached the landing, she heard a muffled scream.

Enormous waves of Jane's terror and panic mingled with the killer's rage and fury washed over Cora. Buckling to her knees just before she reached Jane's door, Cora put her hands on her temples and began building her shield. This process took less than a second with a calm mind, but the barrage of tumbling emotions made it difficult to order her thoughts.

"Jane! Jane!" Linus banged on the door. "Are you okay?"

They heard another muffled scream.

"I can't open that door," Steven said from the floating screen hovering over Cora's bracelet. "He's disabled it somehow."

"I'm coming in," Linus yelled, raising the blaster to the door.

Cora shut out all noises. She concentrated on calming herself and felt her shield strengthen in gradual increments around her mind.

Linus pointed the blaster at the door's side where the electronic lock kept it closed. He fired, but it only bored a tiny hole through the side of the door; it didn't budge.

"Jane! Jane, what's going on?" Linus pummeled the door again.

A moment later, the door slid open and a dark figure slammed Linus into the wall opposite the door and he dropped his blaster as he fell with a thump. The figure took large strides past Cora, who'd just regained her footing and disappeared down the stairs. She studied his retreating shape, wondering what she was looking at. There were no human features. Eyes, ears, nose, and mouth didn't exist. Instead, she observed smooth black skin over his entire body. Cora would've said he was an advanced robot, but she had felt his raw emotions. He was human!

"What was that?" Cora asked in a shaky voice.

"I'll tell you later," Steven said from the floating screen. "Check on Linus, then Jane."

She turned and raced to Linus, who was still unconscious.

"Linus, Linus, wake up," Cora said and turned to Steven. "Show me where the nearest medipad is."

"Go back to the top of the stairs," Steven said.

Cora jumped to her feet and jogged to the stairs. She saw the medipad button before Steven could show her. Pressing a button caused it to eject from the wall and float. Cora pushed it toward Linus.

"Please take care of him," Cora said, a little out of breath. Two probes from the medipad extended to Linus's head and chest, but she didn't wait for the diagnosis. She turned and rushed into Jane's room.

"Jane, are you okay?" she called and paused, taking in the room's state. Everything was a mess. It looked as if the man in the robot suit had waged war with Jane. They'd turned the tables over, knocked the chairs to their sides, and strewn food particles over everything.

Jane lay in the middle of the floor in the fetal position, crying. She wore a thin camisole and sleeping shorts. Cora stepped toward her and pulled her into a hug until her sobs had calmed somewhat.

"What's going on?" Brian said in a raised voice as he rushed into the room wearing a wrinkled business jumpsuit. "Are you okay?"

"I'm fine. What are you doing here?" Cora asked, turning to Brian. "Never mind, something happened to Jane."

"Let me get the medipad," Brian said, jumping to his feet. "Where is it?"

"Where's the medipad?" Cora said, turning to her floating screen, but it was blank.

Jane pointed to the wall, which had a series of family portraits.

Brian found the medipad button and maneuvered it toward Jane. Its probes extended and reached for her head and chest.

"Subject has received trauma to the temple," a dry mechanical voice called.

Cora examined Jane's temple and found the round circle of missing skin about two or three centimeters in diameter. But it reminded her of something. Then she recalled the procedure the EGS performed on her cousin after they captured him.

What was he trying to do? she thought.

"Subject has also received a sedative," the mechanical voice continued. "In addition, the subject's adrenaline is elevated. Will correct the trauma to the temple. A third probe extended from the medipad and sprayed a white foam into the round depression on Jane's temple. A moment later, it evaporated and her skin returned to normal.

Jane had mild bruising on her arms, but the medipad didn't address those. Instead, it withdrew its probes and folded them back into its body. It remained floating next to Jane.

"Let's get her to the sofa," Brian said. They both supported an arm, helping Jane regain her feet, and then walked her to the sofa. Cora spotted Jane's robe at the end of her bed. She retrieved it and helped Jane slip it on.

"Are you up for talking to us?" Cora asked. "Can you tell us what happened?"

"I don't really know," Jane said, tearing up again. "I was asleep. And then my head started hurting. The pain woke me up. When I reached for my head, something heavy settled on my chest and I couldn't breathe. Pushing against whatever was on my chest made the heavy feeling go away. I yelled 'lights' several times, but nothing happened. I stood and tried to make it to the door while kicking and swinging into the dark."

"Did you sense someone in the room with you?" Cora asked.

"Yes, but I couldn't tell where he was," Jane said. "We got tangled up and fell to the floor. Then he put his knee on my chest and tried to drill into my head. But I panicked and used all my strength to send a Reader message to him to 'go away.' He stopped struggling, stood still, but I could feel him fighting my message. Linus was banging on the door, which also spooked him. He backed away from me and stepped out the door."

Agent Taylor stepped into the room supporting Linus, who stumbled while she helped him to a chair opposite the sofa. She wore her gray IPS jumpsuit.

"I understand you had some excitement here," Agent Taylor said, gazing at Cora, Jane, Brian, and Linus. "Are any of you hurt?"

"We used the medipad on Jane," Cora said. "I didn't wait for the other medipad to finish working on Linus."

"I checked him before I entered," Brian said. "He had a mild concussion, but the medipad had finished working on him."

"And the two of you are unharmed?" Agent Taylor asked.

Brian and Cora nodded.

"Would you tell me what happened here?" Agent Taylor asked. "Let me get your consent first." She started the inquiry and asked the three of them to consent to being recorded.

Cora started by saying she'd received a message that someone broke into Jane's home. She also showed the short vid of the stranger walking through the sitting room and hallway.

They all took turns speaking, and Agent Taylor recorded their statements.

"What exactly did he look like?" Agent Taylor asked.

"He looked like a shiny black robot," Jane said with a shiver. "When he touched me, he didn't feel like metal or skin. I can't describe it. But I could feel small bits of his mind. He was human."

"I got a good look at him in the hallway," Cora said. "He was smooth everywhere, as if his skin was flowing. It's difficult to describe. I've never seen anything like it."

"What were you doing here?" Agent Taylor asked, turning to Cora.

Cora paused for a moment, unsure if she should mention Steven.

"Steven Marsh contacted me," Cora said. "The vid I sent you is from Steven."

"Did he contact you two, also?" Agent Taylor asked.

"He showed me the same vid that Cora sent to you," Linus said, nodding.

"Same," Brian nodded.

Cora noted Agent Taylor never asked any questions about Steven's identity.

"Is there anyone else in the house?" Agent Taylor asked, closing her floating screen.

"My parents," Jane said in an alarmed voice. "Why didn't they wake with the commotion?"

"Stay here," Agent Taylor said. "I'll return in a moment." She left the room.

"Remember how Wilma and the rest of her family overslept?" Cora asked.

Jane nodded.

"Do you think the same thing could've happened to Mom and Dad?" Jane asked.

"I think Robot Man sedated your parents," Cora said and furrowed her eyebrows. "What I don't understand is why you woke up?"

"Robot Man?" Jane asked. "Is that what that thing's called?"

"It's what I'm calling him until I know more," Cora said. "So, why did you wake up?"

"Oh, that... it's my body," Jane said with a wry smile. "I have a lot of trouble sleeping, even with a sedative. My guess is he gave me something based on my weight. He got unlucky."

"I'm so relieved you're alive," Linus said, climbing to his feet on shaky legs and making his way to the sofa next to Jane. He hugged her. "I don't know what I would've done if I'd lost you too."

"Do you think this happened to Aria?" Jane said, her fingers trembling as she reached for her temple. "What I don't understand is why?"

I have an idea of what's happening, and who it might be, Cora thought. *But I need more proof.*

"Jane," Cora said. "I think you and your family are still in danger. We should talk to the IPS about additional protection."

"Both of your parents are unconscious," Agent Taylor said, entering the room. "But they're healthy. I use the medipad in their room to check them. They've been sedated, and I can't wake them up. I wouldn't want your home's medipad to do it—you should use something more advanced."

"Can we wait until morning?" Jane asked.

"Yes, I recommend it," Agent Taylor said. "I've programmed the medipad to monitor them throughout the night."

"Out of curiosity, what happened at the Casino Dome?" Brian asked.

"There's an ongoing war between two casino owners," Agent Taylor said with a tired sigh. "Tonight it boiled over into a full laser battle with blasters of all sizes. Several people are dead now. But the dome is unharmed."

"That was so dangerous," Brian said. "If the dome had absorbed the laser blasts, it could've cracked."

"We were able to remove the blasters," Agent Taylor said, running a hand down her face. "But we've been trying to stop the fighting for hours."

For the first time since meeting Agent Taylor, Cora felt sorry for her.

"It's a strange coincidence," Cora said. "The IPS is completely busy at the same time somebody breaks into this home."

"Hmm... What caused the fight?" Brian asked.

"It seems it started with a misunderstanding," Agent Taylor said with a thoughtful expression. "But I don't understand why it escalated so quickly. I'll get the details in the next few days."

"I hope it was a coincidence," Cora said with her eyebrows furrowed. "Because if it's not, it means Robot Man is more powerful than we thought."

CHAPTER 17

After a night of IPS questioning at Jane Spencer's home, Cora and Brian finally stepped through the suite's door. Cora was still in the long-sleeved shirt and pants she'd pulled on at the last minute, and Brian wore his wrinkled business jumpsuit.

"Where have you been?" Aunt Ferna said, jumping to her feet. "We were so worried about you."

Behind her, Benjamin shook his head and rolled his eyes.

"You should've left a message," Aunt Ferna said. "What if something had happened to you?" She met them at the door, grasped Cora's arm and maneuvered her to the dining room table. "Do you want some coffee? Breakfast?"

Cora nodded. Even though her entire body felt heavy, as if she could sleep forever, she almost never turned down coffee. Brian took the next seat and began scrolling the meal crafter's menu. A moment later, two cups of coffee materialized in front of Cora and Brian. A cranberry muffin appeared near Brian while a piece of warm buttered toast turned up in front of Cora. They both took a sip of coffee and Cora exhaled as if her world was returning to normal.

"So, what were you up to last night?" Benjamin asked, taking a sip of coffee.

Brian explained that they'd received a message, ran to Jane's house, and saved her from something that looked like a robot. Aunt Ferna clutched her coffee cup as her face grew white.

"Why in the world would you believe anything from Steven Marsh?" Aunt Ferna said. "He helped Oliver."

Cora raised an eyebrow at that. Aunt Ferna never admitted, at least not out loud, that her precious son had done anything wrong. It was always someone else's fault.

"Steven woke me up in a panic," Cora said. "I've known Steven for more than ten years, and he never panics. He's usually the calm one in control because if there is a *situation*, he created it. I never doubted he was telling the truth."

She bit into her toast enjoying the warmth and crunch.

"Even so, you're just one person," Aunt Ferna said. "What were you supposed to do against an intruder?"

"Well... He asked me to meet Cora," Brian said with a sigh. "When I started arguing, he cut the vidchat. So, I guess after that, he must have asked Linus who went and helped. In Steven's defense, he never intended for her to be alone."

"Linus is armed; I was safe with him," Cora said, trying to stifle a yawn. She turned to Brian. "You eventually showed up."

"Only after I left my office, came to our suite, and discovered you weren't in your room," Brian said with a frown. "That's when I realized things were serious." He turned to Cora. "Everything about this investigation scares me. You could've died."

"In the future, call the IPS," Aunt Ferna said in a firm voice. "I have no idea why Steven thought contacting you would be a better idea."

"The IPS had an issue in the Casino Dome," Cora explained. "It was serious enough that they closed the airlocks between the domes. There was a laser battle between two casino bosses that could've ruptured the dome."

"Laser battle!" Benjamin said. "I hope Omar's safe."

"Even so, he shouldn't have called you," Aunt Ferna continued, ignoring Cora's words.

"After they subdued the fight, they needed to check the dome's stability before they could open the airlocks again."

"That sounds like quite a bit of chaos," Benjamin said. "I'm going to vidchat with him." He turned to Cora. "Happy to have you and Brian safely home." He stepped into his room, and the door closed behind him.

"If I hadn't made plans to meet with some friends, I would stay here," Aunt Ferna said. "But I'm guessing you two are going to catch up on your sleep."

Cora yawned and Brian gazed at her, bleary-eyed.

"I'm going to be spending the day with Omar," Benjamin said, coming back out of his room. "The good news is, he's alright. We have some last-minute details to hash out before we go on our trip." He patted Cora's and Brian's shoulders and left the suite.

"I'm going to check up on you in an hour," Aunt Ferna said. "I expect to find you both snoring."

Cora took another bite of toast.

Her aunt hugged her and left the suite.

"I wondered why we found them both awake and dressed," Cora said with a lopsided smile.

A few minutes later, the door opened. Without turning around, Cora rolled her eyes; she knew who had entered. Steven sat at the table in Benjamin's chair.

"Good morning, all," Steven said in a cheerful tone. "Last night was fun, wasn't it?"

"I'm exhausted Steven," Cora said. "Could we talk later?"

"No," Steven scowled. "You're all in danger. Everyone the... what did you call him?"

"Robot Man," Cora said and shivered at the memory of him.

"This won't take long," Steven said. "Everyone Robot man saw is a potential victim. Together, you stopped him. I don't think he knows who I am, but if he stole military tech, he could find me."

"Maybe we should go back to Tymal," Brian said.

"That's a good idea," Steven said. "If he doesn't think you're a threat, he should leave you alone."

"I'm sorry," Cora said, climbing to her feet. "I'm too tired to discuss this now."

"Please stay," Steven said in a soft voice, grasping her hand. "This is important."

Cora sat, pressing a button on the crafter and a fresh cup of coffee appeared on the table.

"I wanted to discuss the tech that guy was wearing yesterday," Steven said, pointing at Brian's plate. "But first, what type of muffin is that?"

"Cranberry," Brian said, rubbing his face.

"Perfect," Steven said as he scrolled on the crafter's menu and selected coffee and a cranberry muffin. After biting into the warm muffin. He closed his eyes with a small smile. Then he took a sip of coffee.

"Can we please get on with it?" Brian asked, in an irritable tone of voice.

"I missed dinner last night and breakfast this morning," Steven said. "To begin with, that outer skin you saw that looked like fluid is the latest in military tech. It deflects all of our scanning technology. Even though I could see him in the house, our scanners never detected him. That's how he got into the house and disabled the home's AI."

"How do you think he accessed the military suit?" Brian asked.

"I don't know," Steven said. "I can usually poach old military tech, but the newest is difficult to access. What I don't understand is why he didn't use the suit's full invisibility. He should've been able to gain access to Jane's room, kill her, and leave with no evidence."

"He didn't think he needed the precaution," Brian said. "Everyone should have been unconscious."

"I don't know. Jane didn't have enough sedative to stay asleep. Maybe he wanted to scare her," Cora said. "It was important to him to terrorize her first. He may have used the suit's full invisibility when he entered the Meadcroft house. He didn't need to scare Aria."

"We may never know," Steven said. "But one thing I'm sure of; these attacks are personal or linked."

"Now that he's seen Cora and Linus, will their murders be personal, too?" Brian asked in a raised voice.

Cora exchanged glances with Brian, but she didn't know what to say.

"The second thing we should discuss is, what was he doing there?" Steven asked, ignoring Brian. "He was trying to insert a neurowall. It's actually a painful process, but usually the person inserting the neurowall uses a local anesthetic. Of course, he didn't do that last night. The pain woke Jane last night. I think that was a mistake on his part."

"What I don't understand is when the IPS examined Aria and Drew, there was no evidence of a neurowall," Cora said, rubbing her face to stay awake.

"He could've used a bonding spray to heal their temples," Steven said. "More importantly, there's a type of neurowall which dissolves within twenty-four hours after it's installed. Unfortunately, if you're Askovian and use your abilities during that twenty-four-hour period, it causes death."

"Aria was a Reader and Drew was a Mover," Brian said with a heavy sigh. "Cora is a Feeler. She's in danger."

"How does it work?" Cora asked, shaken at Brian's words.

"It's coated with callenium," Steven said.

"A perfect reflector," Cora said, remembering the lunar surface tour several days ago.

"Yes, it causes specific brain waves to bounce and amplify within the brain," Steven said. "When Askovian abilities create these waves, they destroy the brain." He downed the last of his coffee.

"It must be painful," Cora said as an image of Drew clutching his head before falling crossed her mind. "He wants to cause as much pain as possible. That's somebody who's really angry."

"Exactly," Steven said.

"This points to Xavier Varney," Cora said. "The accident five years ago caused the loss of his family. This would make him angry and link Aria, Drew, and Jane. The only problem is I haven't been able to find Xavier in Tymal."

"I couldn't find him in Lunar City," Steven said. "I also checked other major Askov cities on Earth."

"Maybe it's a relative who is doing this," Brian said. "On Xavier's behalf."

"I wondered about that too," Steven said, taking a bite of his cranberry muffin. "But his cousins don't appear to have the skills to steal military tech. One is an artist and the other a sculptor."

"I almost forgot," Cora said with a yawn. "Yesterday, when I mentioned your name to Agent Taylor, she never asked any follow-up questions. Are you working for the IPS?"

"I'm more of a consultant," Steven said with a wry smile. "In order to stay out of a penal colony, they protect me from the EGS and I provide them with valuable information."

"So, you give the IPS information about us," Brian said. "That makes you untrustworthy."

"I am so tired," Cora said, trying to avert an argument. "Can we continue this conversation later?"

"I stopped by to drop off those little tidbits of information," Steven turned to Brian and scowled. "The next time I tell you that something's life and death. Believe me. When you decided not to show up, you could have killed Cora."

"I could have killed her!" Brian yelled, jumping to his feet. "This is your fault. You should have called the IPS."

"Are you completely stupid?" Steven asked in a raised voice. "Agent Taylor explained several times, there was an incident in the Casino Dome."

"Well, how was I supposed to know you were serious?" Brian said in a tense voice. "I don't like you associating with Cora. Every time you're involved, something bad happens. You're banned from talking to her."

Steven guffawed.

"Okay, Brian," Cora massaged her temples. "I think we're both too tired. It's time for us to get some sleep."

Brian stormed into his bedroom.

Cora watched him go and sighed.

"Do you have to rile him up?" Cora asked, turning to Steven.

He smirked, popped the last bite of cranberry muffin in his mouth, and climbed to his feet.

"I'll contact you later when I find out more," Steven said as he sauntered out of the room.

Cora sat alone in the dining room, wondering about the killer's next move. Given that he went after Aria, Drew, and Jane, was he going to go after Jane again? Porter? Linus?

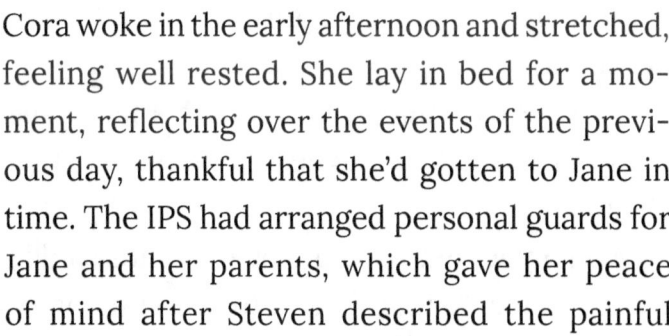

Cora woke in the early afternoon and stretched, feeling well rested. She lay in bed for a moment, reflecting over the events of the previous day, thankful that she'd gotten to Jane in time. The IPS had arranged personal guards for Jane and her parents, which gave her peace of mind after Steven described the painful death she would've endured. For a moment, she wondered if two human IPS agents would be enough. Especially if Robot Man could turn invisible.

She rolled out of bed, ambled to the bathroom, showered, and changed. Then she stepped into the living and dining room of the suite. Using her abilities, she realized she was by herself.

Did Brian get any sleep? she thought. *Or did he sleep fewer hours?*

She could vidchat him, but what would she say? If she could tell him... What? She sighed, making her way to the dining room table for a lasagna full of lunar vegetables.

"Hmm... Tasty," Cora said. I'll ask Aunt Ferna which ingredients she used for the crafter. Her comm bracelet chimed, and she glanced at the name and opened a floating screen.

"How are you doing?" Cora asked with food in her mouth.

Linus didn't smile and rubbed his face. The bags under his eyes suggested he hadn't slept at all.

"Would you mind coming over?" Linus said in a tired voice. "I really need to tell you something. I don't want to hide anything from you."

"Of course," Cora said. "Let me finish my lunch, and I'll be over in about thirty minutes."

"I'll wait," Linus said, and the screen went dark.

Cora finished her food, took the antigrav lift to the ground floor, and stepped out onto the bright pathway. Gazing through the dome's ceiling, she studied the Earth's quarter phase. It resulted in lower ambient light from outside, but simulated sunlight brightened the dome. She followed the lighted walkway to Linus's house. Soon she stood at the front door and waited, expecting the home's AI to greet her. Instead, the door opened and Linus stood behind it.

"Come in, please," Linus said in a low voice. He still wore his pajamas from last night, and his eyes were bloodshot, as if he'd been crying. For the first time since she'd met Linus, she felt sorry for him.

Cora used her abilities and only sensed Linus in the house. Following him through the main hallway, they turned into a family game room. It was an unusual room with four groups of two plush overstuffed chairs and a small round table along the edge of the room. A large floating games table positioned in the center of the room featured a floating rack with various clubs, mallets, and paddles.

She lowered onto one of the chairs, and he sat opposite. Cora gazed at a series of balls arranged on the floating table.

"Would you like something to drink or eat?" Linus asked.

Cora shook her head. "What did you want to talk about?"

"I just want you to know everything," he said with a sniffle. "Last night or this morning, I realized why that thing attacked Aria, Drew, and Jane. It's because of me, isn't it? This has to do with me crashing into that Original's homestead."

"That's what I think, too," she said in a soft voice, understanding how guilty he must feel.

"You already knew?" he asked with a heavy sigh.

She nodded. "I figured some of it out, but could you tell me more about your friendships with the others?"

"Seven years ago, when Aria was eighteen, and I was nineteen, I fell in love with her," He said and cleared his throat. "But she never loved me. She always wanted Drew. I did what I could to ignore them, but over time, I grew to hate

Drew. Trying to win her made me reckless. It was dumb, but I thought my clipper antics would finally get her attention."

"Is that what happened the day of the accident?" she asked.

"Yeah, it was a stunt I'd done a million times before," he said. "But something broke on my clipper that day, and I lost control. I ejected in time, but my clipper crashed into their home."

They both remained silent for a moment.

"You must miss Aria," Cora said, trying to break the silence.

"The people dying were also involved in that race," Linus said, pursing his lips. "Well, except for Aria. But now I know why somebody killed her. Whoever did it knew I was in love with her. They wanted to hurt me."

"Did you tell anybody about your feelings for Aria?" she asked.

"Yeah. Porter, but he wouldn't tell," he said. "I trust him."

He doesn't seem the type to tell, she thought.

"I've been wondering if Porter could be the killer," she said, trying to gauge his emotions. "He spends a lot of time with the Originals."

"That's impossible," he said in a raised voice. "I've known Porter since we were seventeen years old. He's solid and dependable. I can't even imagine him doing something so heinous."

"But he's the only other person you told," she said.

"We were friends for years, until that accident," he said. "It fractured our group, and nobody wanted to spend time with me. Aria refused to acknowledge me. Jane and Drew decreased their time with me. Even Porter disappeared for a while, although he was working on his business. I think I reminded them of the deaths they were associated with."

Cora sensed Linus's deep despair.

"What about your parents?" she asked.

"They don't really care if I'm here or not," he said in a level voice. "They're focused on their Lunar City council seats and getting reelected. When I had that accident, I almost derailed their entire careers."

"Just because your parents are running for Lunar City council, doesn't mean they don't care about you," she said.

"You'd be surprised," he said. "My five-year-probation ended a few months ago, and I started getting death threats. You see,. I never had any jail time. My parents lost a lot of credibility and blamed me. Rightfully."

"Is that why you started carrying a blaster?" she asked.

"Yeah," he said. "The thing is, I don't even blame them."

"Do your parents get threats?" she asked.

Linus shook his head. "But they've started using a private security service just in case."

"Well, you still have friends," she said.

"The Originals are aggressive and fearful around me," he said with a mirthless laugh. "Most Askovs don't want to be associated with me. Really, nobody in Lunar City wants me here." He stared at the ceiling as if gathering his thoughts before continuing. "There's a cruiser leaving for Anteros, in a few days. I've already bought my ticket and I'm packed and ready to go."

"What about the killer?" she asked.

"I can't leave before he's caught," he said in a determined tone. "If the IPS hasn't caught him before the ship leaves, I'll cancel my trip. But if there's anything I can do to help you or the IPS, please let me know."

"When I asked about your blaster a couple of weeks ago, you said it was protection for a trip," Cora said. "Is this what you were referring to?"

"Yeah," he shrugged. "I thought I'd start my own farm outside of Anteros. It's rumored to have lots of outlaws. In any case, a little protection wouldn't hurt."

"Did anybody know you were going to leave?" she asked.

"Porter. But I asked him not to tell anybody else," he said.

Cora furrowed her eyebrows.

"My original plan was to slink away, unnoticed," he said. "Aria and Drew should have been on Earth on a vacation. Jane wouldn't care what happened to me. Porter was my last remaining friend, and I told him."

"I wish I could go back in time and reverse the accident," he said. "But I was too dumb."

"What happened after the Varney family died?" she asked.

"We had to hire extra guards, which included several robots and a few IPS agents because of the death threats," Linus said with a heavy sigh.

"How long did the IPS guard you and your parents?" Cora asked.

"Six months at first," Linus said. "Then the council agreed I should at least go to trial. I was found guilty, and I made a public apology. When the judge announced a sentence of five years' probation, that caused more riots. We needed more protection, which lasted about four years. That's when we stopped receiving death threats. But I don't feel comfortable when I'm alone in public."

"To tell you the truth," Cora said. "I don't think we're going to figure out who's behind this before the cruiser leaves. After I saw the high-tech equipment on Robot Man, I realized I was out of my depth."

CHAPTER 18

Cora and Brian sat next to each other in his bedroom on a tiny sofa facing a coffee table. A wall vid screen very similar to the one Jane had in her home, showed a live view of the landscape outside of Lunar City as occasional meteorites impacted the surface of the Moon.

"First, I want to apologize for not talking to you these past few days," Brian said in a quiet voice, wearing a crisp new business jumpsuit for work.

"You don't need to apologize," Cora said in a wobbly voice as she sensed the direction of this conversation. She still wore her wrinkled pajamas.

She used her abilities to sense Brian's emotions, but she only sensed waves of sadness and regret.

"I needed time to think about what I want from our relationship," he said. "I've decided to go to Mars with my father."

Cora's face fell as tears streamed down her cheeks. They held each other on the sofa for a few minutes.

"I'd hoped we could grow closer," she said in a shaky voice. "Over the last few years, I've come to rely on your friendship. It's invaluable to me."

"And that's the problem," he said, wiping tears from his eyes. "You want us to continue as friends? But I love you and I want more from our relationship than friendship. I want to marry you and have children. I can't continue only being your friend."

"But, but I just need more time," she said, stumbling over her words.

"You can have all the time that you want," he said. "You'll have three or four years to think about it. And when I come back, if you're interested in a deeper relationship, I'll be open to that. If not, then I think it's for the best that we separate."

She wiped her eyes for a few minutes. Staring at the vid screen of the lunar landscape, she tried to take everything in.

"What are you going to do when you're on Mars?" she asked in a low voice.

"I'm going to expand my business into Martian law," he said in a steady voice. "I have clients here who need help to navigate the law and the IPS. More clients based on Mars will need my help. I'm nervous but excited about creating something for myself."

She sensed his sadness and also his love, but her stomach wobbled with her tumbling feelings. The thought of him moving away weighed on her. Maybe if he stayed longer, she'd have a chance to sift through her feelings.

"I'm leaving in about a week," he said. "I hope Robot Man is caught, otherwise I won't feel comfortable leaving you here." He turned to face her. "Promise me that after I leave, you'll go back to Tymal. I really feel you're in danger."

Cora nodded but didn't reply. She knew she couldn't leave with a killer running around. He hadn't finished killing.

"I'm going to miss you so much," she said with a long hug. "I don't know what I'm going to do without you being a simple vidchat away."

About thirty minutes later, Cora sat at the suite's dining room table staring at her coffee cup until it grew cold. Brian and his dad had left earlier to run their errands and Aunt Ferna was sleeping, having come in late last night.

"Good morning," Aunt Ferna said in a cheery voice.

Cora jumped. She'd been so lost in thought she hadn't heard Aunt Ferna's footsteps. Somehow, the sight of Aunt Ferna reminded her of the countless times she'd been there for comfort. Cora burst into tears, and Aunt Ferna strode to her side, moved a chair closer, and embraced her.

"Do you want to talk about it?" Aunt Ferna asked in a gentle voice.

Cora wiped her eyes, sensing Aunt Ferna's concern, and confided in her. She explained Brian loved her, but she didn't know how she felt.

"Did you know he felt that way?"

"I suspected as much."

"It feels too fast." Cora said, frowning. "I don't know..."

"I know this is confusing, dear," Aunt Ferna said with a gentle hug. "Maybe you two just need time to work on this."

"That's one thing we don't have," Cora said. "He's leaving with his Dad. I don't want him to go, even though it's best for him."

"I understand that," Aunt Ferna said, and suddenly grinned. "But I have a plan, my dear."

"You make me nervous when you get that look in your eyes," Cora said with a reluctant smile.

"What we're going to do is visit a Seer," Aunt Ferna said, beaming.

"Oh, no. Not Hilda again," Cora said with a frown. "She's a fraud just like her sister Etta." Cora had met Etta many months ago. She claimed to have Seer abilities, but Oliver had hired her to mislead Harold.

"No, dear," Aunt Ferna said with a sigh. "I think you're jumping to conclusions. Let's say you're right and she's a fraud. If that's the case, we can ignore whatever she says. But if she has the power, what she says could change your life."

Cora wrinkled her forehead, trying to sort through Aunt Ferna's logic.

"I don't want to go," Cora said.

"I know, dear, but remember, auntie knows best," Aunt Ferna said. "Have you eaten breakfast?"

Cora turned to the meal crafter and selected synthetic scrambled eggs and bacon. Aunt Ferna selected an iced bun and a cup of tea.

"Remember, I felt my Oliver pass away a few months ago," Aunt Ferna said, slicing a piece of her iced bun, stabbing it with a fork, and swallowing. "Warmed iced buns for breakfast are the best."

Cora washed down a bit of her eggs and bacon with coffee, surprised. She'd often heard Aunt Ferna say unusual things, and she paid attention, as her aunt's hunches were usually right.

"When I had my reading with Hilda, she confirmed it," Aunt Ferna said.

"Yeah, but how'd Hilda really know?" Cora asked, taking another sip.

"Since we've been here in Lunar City, I've heard rumors from my friends," Aunt Ferna said. "They know quite a bit about how the IPS and the EGS operate. The root of the problem is that many Originals are quite paranoid about the power surrounding Askovs. They're referring to our abilities and our financial and political influence. They're afraid over time the Originals will be slaves to the Askovs."

This sounded like the opposite of Porter's lecture in the Originals Dome, Cora thought.

"The EGS and IPS are using captured Askovs as test subjects," Aunt Ferna said. "The point of these tests is to create technology to protect the Originals."

Cora patted her aunt's hand.

"I think Hilda has actual powers," Aunt Ferna said. "She explained what happened to Oliver and how he died."

"Have you considered that Hilda simply heard the rumors?" Cora asked.

"True, but it won't hurt to hear her out," Aunt Ferna said, not even bothering with any logic this time. "Also, visiting her could distract you from your troubles with Brian."

Cora sighed, accepting defeat.

"Now, you change out of your pajamas, and let's get out of here in about thirty minutes," Aunt Ferna said, patting Cora's hand.

About forty-five minutes later, Cora and Aunt Ferna strolled through the Askov neighborhood and stopped at a flat gray front door. It slid open onto an enclosed walkway that ended in a tiny garden with a fountain. As they stepped through, she gazed at the small apartment complex that reminded her of something she'd find in Tymal. The small garden at the end of the walkway included well-maintained clipped grass, flowers, and a statue of Askae. It must've been expensive to manage all of those natural resources.

As she stood gazing at the water fountain, a voice from behind made her jump. Since she was shielded, she hadn't noticed Hilda approach from behind.

"Thank you so much for coming to visit me. I'm Hilda," she said, facing Cora. Hilda could have been Etta's twin, except that she was a few years younger, with graying hair and a few wrinkles. They had the same green eyes, but Hilda's seemed to look into Cora's soul.

"Hilda," Aunt Ferna said, leaning in for a quick hug. "I brought my niece, Cora, for a seeing."

"I'm glad you trusted me enough to give you a seeing," Hilda said. "Please come with me. We'll have more privacy in my apartment."

Hilda turned and led the way as Cora and Aunt Ferna followed. They stepped into a cheery little apartment with a living room that displayed a floral print sofa with a coffee table. They continued into the dining room, which had a small square table and four chairs.

"Would you like something to eat?" Hilda asked as the three women took their seats.

Cora and Aunt Ferna nodded.

"I have tea and these amazing raspberry cookies," Hilda said, selecting buttons on the crafter at the center of the dining room table. A moment later, a hot cup of tea appeared next to Cora, Hilda, and Aunt Ferna, while a plate of raspberry cookies materialized toward the center of the table.

"What do we do for a Seeing?" Cora asked. "Do we hold hands? Do you look at my palm?"

Hilda chuckled, making a light, musical sound.

"No, nothing like that," Hilda said. "That's more for drama or performance. I only need to be in your space long enough to see. Sometimes I see your future, your past, or something significant happening now. It depends on what you'll let me see."

"I know your sister Etta," Cora said, crossing her arms.

"Well, that explains everything," Hilda said. "Most people I meet who've already met my sister assume that I'm a fraud as well. I don't have any way to convince you I'm not a fraud. But I'll make you this promise—I'll only tell you the truth."

"Can you explain a little how your Seer ability works?" Cora asked, taking a sip of tea.

"It's a little like being a Reader, Listener, and Viewer, except that I'm not bound by time," Hilda said. "I can hear thoughts from a long time ago or from the future. I can see events relevant to you in the past, present, or future. That's because I'm only focusing on you." She paused, exchanging a glance with Aunt Ferna. "There's a chance I won't get anything from you. I don't consider Seeing an ability. It's more of a gift because I can't control it."

"Listeners can hear tectonic plates shifting kilometers below the Earth's surface," Cora said. "They could help scientists determine the next earthquake. Is it like that?"

"Not quite," Hilda said. "I'm not bound by time. If that shift in the tectonic plate will happen ten years in the future and would affect the person who asked for my help. I'd hear the rumble and see the earthquake."

"So, we just sit here and talk?" Cora asked, furrowing her eyebrows.

"Absolutely," Hilda said. "What brings you here today?"

"I'm afraid, I insisted," Aunt Ferna said with a mouth full of cookie. "She's had a break in her relationship. I thought you could help."

"Can you tell me about it?" Hilda asked in a gentle tone.

"I had a friendship with Brian," Cora said.

"Do you mean Brian Farris?" Hilda asked, interrupting Cora.

"Yes. Do you know him?" Cora asked.

"I know of him," Hilda said. "But please continue."

"We had a talk this morning, and it seems our friendship is over," Cora said, having difficulty talking about it with a stranger.

Hilda blinked, and her eyes changed to deep pools of green. Cora felt the Seer could peer into her soul.

"You're in grave danger," Hilda said in a low, resonating voice. "Someone wants to kill you."

"Do you know who he is?" Cora asked, as a frisson of fear raced down her back.

"No, I don't," Hilda said, her eyes boring into Cora's. "But you already know who it is. Or you'll figure out who it is today or tomorrow."

"Where can she go to stay safe?" Aunt Ferna asked in a raised voice. "Should we go back to Tymal?"

"It won't matter if you leave Lunar City or stay," Hilda said with the same low, dark voice. "This person is going to try to kill you. They're determined. The only way to save yourself is to figure out who he or she is. Also, get as much help as possible. I mean, use all of your friends, the IPS, and even the EGS."

"Are there some places where she'll be safer than others?" Aunt Ferna asked as worry marred her face.

"As long as she's never alone outside of her suite, she'll be safe," Hilda said with an eerie expression.

Cora shivered.

"The murderer needs to get you alone," Hilda said in an urgent voice. "Make sure you're not alone."

"So, is it possible that we've already met?" Cora asked, her fingers trembling.

"I don't know," Hilda said as her voice returned to normal. "The only thing I know for certain is that the killer is going to try to kill you soon."

"What if you go to the IPS now?" Aunt Ferna asked, grasping Cora's hand.

"How will that work if I don't know who I'm looking for?" Cora asked. "I don't even have proof."

"Are there any other steps Cora can take to stay safe?" Aunt Ferna asked.

"I don't know," Hilda said. "I can't see anything now."

"Is anybody else in danger?" Cora asked.

"I don't know," Hilda said. "Are you thinking of someone?"

"Yes," Cora said. "Jane Spencer."

"I would need to meet her," Hilda said. "And she'd have to be open to my seeing."

"Oh, this is disturbing," Aunt Ferna said. "I'm going to talk to Benjamin immediately and start looking into taking a shuttle to Tymal tomorrow."

"It won't matter if we stay or if we leave," Cora said in a solemn voice. "He's coming after me."

CHAPTER 19

Cora strolled into Central Park in a comfortable short sleeved soft-pink dress that reached her knees. Following a trail through the park, she veered to the right up a low hill. Eventually, she ended at a seating area at the top of a visitor's section.

At the top of the hill, she reached a flat area with a water fountain in the center. She glanced at a ring of seven benches surrounded by foliage that blocked the view of the lower park areas. Peering at the dome overhead, she gazed at the three-quarter Earth phase with the stars in the background. A satisfied smile covered her face as she enjoyed the sight.

"Cora. There you are," Porter said, approaching her. He gave her a quick hug. "I feel I should apologize." He said right away. "Last time we met, I could've been kinder when I was explaining how the Originals live. I could see you were uncomfortable and we should have left earlier."

"Think nothing of it," Cora said with a small smile. "It was instructive to see how Originals live." She gestured to the nearest bench, and they took a seat. "I only have a few questions, so I won't keep you very long."

Cora lowered her shield in small increments. She normally didn't do that in a public space, but they were alone at the moment.

"You can ask as many questions as you want," he said in a serious tone. "I want to find out what happened to Aria and now Jane."

"Yes, that was very disturbing," she said with a frown.

"What exactly happened?" he asked. "I've only heard bits and pieces."

Cora explained how she entered Jane's house and found a man wearing military armor who tried to harm Jane.

Porter scowled.

"I can't believe things are this bad," he said. "Who is so desperate that they'd want to harm Jane?"

"That's part of what I want to talk to you about," she said. "Robot Man wore a shiny black covering that appeared to be advanced military tech. Do you know somebody with advanced programming skills? Somebody at your company?"

"Robot Man?" he asked.

"That's my nickname for him, until I figure out who he is," she said with a lopsided smile.

"Well, yes and no," he said with halting words. "Everybody I work with is a pretty good programmer. That's why I hired them. But that doesn't mean we'd harm Jane. I don't think anybody in my company even knows Jane, except for me and Gavin.

Cora reflected on the conversation she'd had with Linus about how some of the evidence pointed to Porter.

"How well do you know Jane?" she asked. "For example, did you ever date? Is there something you two have in common?"

"I've never dated Jane," he said with a chuckle. "She was never my type—too bossy. But I still don't hate her. We used to race our clippers every weekend. She just struck me as a kid. It was her sister Aria everybody was half in love with. But I know Linus loved her. In the end, Aria chose Drew."

Cora sensed he was telling the truth. *Is this another dead end?* she thought.

"Have you come across advanced programmers here in Lunar City?" she asked. "In conferences? On Earth?" Cora asked.

"Yes, of course," he said. "I encounter advanced programmers in every single conference, whenever I meet with potential clients, or by chance at the Lunar Bakery. I've probably met hundreds of programmers this year. Plenty of them were advanced programmers."

"I'm trying to narrow down who could qualify," Cora said. "But there're so many programmers."

"By the way, you're also an advanced programmer," Porter said with a slight smile.

"I don't consider myself advanced," she said with a chuckle, thinking of Steven Marsh.

"I've been playing with Mystery Adventures for the past few weeks," he said. "And I still haven't figured out an answer to any of your puzzles without asking the AI to give me a hint." He chuckled.

"That's not advanced programming," she said. "That's careful planning on my part."

"A lot of programming is careful planning," he said.

"What about the credits you owed Drew?" she asked.

"Well, I don't see what that has to do with anything," he said. "But I've arranged to give the credits to Drew's parents. Why do you ask?"

"I'm trying to figure out who'd hate Aria, Drew, and Jane enough to commit murder," she said.

"So, I'm a suspect," he said with a scowl. "And why exactly would I do that?"

"I don't know," she said, detecting his increased irritation. "You're connected by that accident that killed the Varney family, but the obvious suspect has disappeared. I thought I'd try to see if I could find other motives."

"Xavier Varney," he said, sighing. "What a horrible day. I wish we could take it back."

Cora felt his irritation melt into a deep sadness.

"Did you know him?" she asked.

"No. Never met him before," he said. "Afterwards... Our lawyers asked us not to communicate with him."

"Did you know Linus's planning to leave Lunar City?" she asked.

"I shouldn't be surprised you found out," he said with a dry chuckle. "He told me a while ago he's planning to leave, but he asked me not to tell."

"Did you tell anyone?" she asked.

He shook his head.

"What happened to you after the accident?" Cora asked.

"I thought we were all going to prison at first," he asked. "Linus's family needed round-the-clock armed guards. But a few weeks in, and everyone focused only on Linus. I stayed inside as much as possible, finishing up a project that later turned into the business I have today. With time, everyone forgot about me, Jane, and Drew."

"On a different topic, I was wondering—" Cora said.

"Hey, Porter," Gavin said, interrupting their conversation. "What are you doing here?"

Cora didn't have her shield up as Gavin approached them. The very first thing she noticed was she couldn't read Gavin's emotions. He wore a neurowall.

"Hey, man," Porter turned to Gavin.

"I'm sorry to interrupt," Gavin said in a serious voice. "We're having a problem at work, and we need you as soon as possible."

"I'm not going anywhere," Porter said with his eyebrows furrowed. "I just discovered I'm the prime suspect in Cora's investigation."

She detected his increasing irritation, which coincided with Gavin joining the conversation.

"Investigation?" Gavin said with a condescending chortle. "Oh, yes. You're looking into Aria's murder. I can assure you Porter is innocent."

"I think Cora was about to ask another question," Porter said, turning to Cora.

She took her time examining Porter's emotions, which flowed between irritation, anger, and sorrow.

"Now that you're here, I'd like to ask you a few questions," she said.

"Okay," Gavin shrugged. "But you're wasting your time."

"Did you know the Varney family?" Cora asked. "They're the family who—"

"Yes, I knew of them, but not personally," Gavin said, cutting her off and setting his mouth in a grim line. "What does this have to do with anything?"

"I think it's not a coincidence that Aria, Drew, and Jane were murdered or attacked," Cora said. "That incident connects everyone."

She paused, unsure of what to ask next.

Is *he covering for Porter?* she thought. Is *Porter covering for him?*

"Do you know any advanced programmers?" Cora asked.

"I know hundreds of advanced programmers," Gavin said and smirked. "Why do you ask?"

"The person who attacked Jane wore a lot of military tech," Cora said, trying to gauge Gavin's facial expressions. "That'd require advanced programming to steal."

"*Steal* military tech..." Gavin lapsed into silence for a moment. "I hadn't thought of it that way."

"We both know lots of advanced programmers," Porter said. "I don't think this line of questioning will reveal any more information."

"I've reached a dead end," Cora said, nodding.

"So, are there any more questions?" Porter asked.

"No, I think that's it," Cora said, standing. "Thank you for your time. Also thank you, Gavin."

Porter stood with her. She nodded to both men, turned, and left.

Gavin never asked what happened to Jane, Cora thought.

Later that evening, Cora turned her investigation to Gavin. The real stumbling block with Gavin being Aria's murderer was that the killer installed her neurowall the night before. But he was in Tymal. Also, it was a little odd that he wore a neurowall, but several Originals had one installed for self-defense. She thought it wouldn't hurt to look into him, anyway.

After an hour of looking through the Net, she noticed something strange. All the information about Gavin Smith started five years ago. She couldn't find any information about him older than that. She found evidence of his birth, schooling, parents, and siblings. However, a deep dive into his background showed that none of the information was dated beyond five years.

A fresh idea crossed her mind, and she turned to Xavier Varney. She found information about his birth in Tymal, his family, schooling, and work. It all stopped abruptly five years ago. It was as if he didn't exist any longer. Xavier had a slender face with platinum blond hair and pale blue eyes.

Somehow, Xavier Varney is Gavin Smith, Cora thought with a grim smile. *But the two men look so different.*

She studied Xavier and Gavin's images side-by-side. Gavin had a fuller face with a receding hairline, brown hair, and hazel eyes. A vidchat interrupted her thoughts. Glancing at her comm bracelet, she noticed it was from Porter. She opened a floating screen, starting the vidchat.

"Hey," Porter said. "I just thought about something related to advanced programmers. I think I found a military link here at work. Could you meet me?"

"It's a little late for me," Cora said as a tightness settled in her chest. She wished she could gauge Porter's emotions. "Can I meet you tomorrow morning instead?"

"Oh, sure," Porter said. "Tomorrow is fine." He ended the vidchat.

Cora hurried to open a brand-new window and started a vidchat with Steven.

"I think Gavin Smith is Xavier Varney," Cora said.

"No," Steven said. "I checked Gavin Smith a week or two ago. He's clean. And he looks nothing like Xavier."

"I checked his source information on the Net," she said in a serious tone. "None of it is older than five years. Gavin didn't exist until five years ago. Not sure why he looks so different now."

"The source..." he said. "I must be slipping. Why didn't I do that check? I already dismissed him."

"Gavin or Xavier have the best motive to kill Drew and Jane," she said with insistence. "He killed Aria because he knew Linus was in love with her. Linus admitted to telling Porter, who shares everything with Gavin."

"But they look nothing alike," he said. "Wait... Gavin was in Tymal when Aria's neurowall was installed."

"I know," she frowned. "But I think Porter might be helping him."

"It's possible," he said, examining something off screen. "In a moment we'll have seventeen segments of vids from the morning Aria died. Maybe we'll see something."

"I don't know..." she said, staring at the wall for a moment. "The evidence suggests it, but Porter's been very open with me. On the other hand, Gavin interrupted my discussions with Porter multiple times. He travels to Earth once or twice a month, which gives him access to the EGS and military tech."

"Wait," he said as a chime sounded in the background. A moment later, a new floating screen appeared with a vid. The time started a few minutes before Aria's passing. A crowd exited the shuttle. It appeared as if Gavin materialized out of thin air among the crowd. Steven and Cora watched a few more vids from different angles in the spaceport. Some corroborated the first vid, and some were at the wrong angle to capture the crowd.

"Was he wearing his Robot Man suit?" she asked.

"I think so," he said. "Okay, watch this vid."

The screen showed the same crowd from a new angle. The crowd jostled around an invisible object and a second later, Gavin appeared.

"He actually sneaked in, blending with the crowd," she said. "He was already in Lunar City when Aria passed away."

"None of our sensors picked up Gavin until he appeared with that crowd," he said. "We can't see him in full invisibility mode, meaning he can come and go as he wants."

She shivered.

"I think you're in danger," Steven said in a panicky voice. "I'll send the IPS, but it'll take time."

"The IPS might be a little overkill," Cora said, shaking her head. "But, now that I think about it, Porter and I just had a vidchat, and he asked me to come to his office."

"Hold on a minute," he said, turning to something off screen. After a full minute, he turned to face her. "Porter didn't contact you. I think that was the killer."

"Are you sure?" she asked. "He looked like Porter, sounded like him, and even moved like him."

"I'm continuously monitoring Linus, Jane, and Porter to keep them safe," he said. "Porter never contacted you. He's at home working on some code and hasn't started a vidchat to anyone all evening."

"He could have created programs to trick your surveillance," she said.

"No, I don't think so," he said with a smirk. "He's advanced, but he's not a hacker. I'm not admitting to anything, but it'd be difficult to avoid my... observation software."

"Could it have been someone else at his office?" she asked, shifting uncomfortably in her seat. Steven had taught her how to hack into other AIs when they were at school. She didn't doubt his surveillance code.

"No, I'm tracking all communication from his workplace, too," he said. "I think you're in danger. Leave the suite now and visit Aunt Ferna's friends. Do you know where they are?"

"Y-Yes," she said, as her chest tightened. "But I don't think leaving will make me safer. Once I step outside the suite, I could be more vulnerable."

Hilda said, "as long as she's never alone outside of her suite, she'll be safe," she thought. She couldn't tell Steven she was relying on a Seer's words.

Cora heard three knocks on the door and froze in place.

CHAPTER 20

Three more knocks sounded at the entrance to her suite. Cora's heart thumped in her ears; certain she knew who was on the other side of the door. She pressed the button on her comm bracelet, trying to reach Steven, surprised that the floating screen for the vid-chat remained blank.

"Pull yourself together," Cora said to herself in a shaky voice. She closed the blank screen and started recording herself inside the suite. Hoping Steven would realize she needed help, she opened another floating window and tried to call Aunt Ferna, Brian, Benjamin, and the IPS. That's when she realized the murderer had cut off her access to the Net.

Suddenly, the door slid open, but nobody was there. Cora trembled. She kept her shield lowered to gauge the killer's erratic emotions,

alternating between fury, disgust, and something... Bravery? Detecting hints of insanity,
she wondered how long she could stall before
someone rescued her.

"Gavin, I know it's you," she said in a quaking
voice. "I can feel your emotions. Your anger and
also your fear."

She jumped as Gavin's laughter came from a
spot much closer to her than she'd thought.

A moment later, he appeared on the other
side of the dining room table covered in that
black, flowing metal. He raised one arm and
pressed a button on the suit. The entire suit
faded away. Gavin stood in front of her, dressed
in the business jumpsuit he'd been wearing earlier in the afternoon.

"What are you doing here?" Cora asked in a
squeaky voice.

"I underestimated you," Gavin said with a lopsided smile. "Actually, I like you. I wish I didn't
have to kill you."

A stone settled in Cora's stomach as she
sensed his truth. He pursued a goal, and Cora
stood in the way.

"Is this about the accident that killed your
family?" she asked.

"It wasn't an accident," he said, taking two steps around the dining table. "They'd raced over my farm dozens of times even though I threatened to call IPS. They refused to stop and killed my family. Now I've killed Drew. My next targets are Jane, Linus, and Porter."

"You look so different from Xavier," she said, circling in the opposite direction. "How did you do that?"

"Very expensive surgery," he said, taking two more steps. "I needed to pass facial recognition for my new identity."

"You've been planning this a while then," she said, backing away from him.

"Five long years," he grinned. "Then I heard Linus planned to run away, but I'll kill him last."

"How did you get everyone at the spaceport at the same time?" she asked.

"Easy, Linus follows Aria everywhere, and I asked Porter to pick me up." He chuckled. "Then I intercepted Aria and Jane's comm messages, making them meet at the spaceport." Taking another two steps, he stood at her original spot. "I'm going to make Linus watch all his friends die, just like I watched my family die."

"But Aria wasn't part of the race. You didn't need to kill her," she said, taking one step further around the table.

Gavin   grinned,   continuing   their cat-and-mouse game.

Cora paced, trying to keep the table between them.

"How did you kill her?" Cora asked.

"Wearing my tactical armor, I walked into the Meadcroft's home," he said. "I added a slow acting but powerful sedative to their drinks—I had to wait for the dad, though. Once they were all asleep, I entered Wilma's bedroom where Aria slept and installed a military grade dissolving neurowall."

"How did you get that tactical armor?" she asked, taking her first step away from the table toward the front door.

"I know you're stalling, but it doesn't matter. Nobody's coming," he said casually, leaning on the dining room table. "I've been stealing from the EGS for years. I usually take small gadgets or old tech. But somebody was dumb enough to send a full suit of military grade tactical armor to the EGS. I think they planned to use it in the future for riot control or something. This is a prototype, but it works perfectly. I haven't had a single problem with it."

"I notice I can sense your emotions now," Cora continued with another step toward the exit. "But this afternoon, in the park, I couldn't feel anything."

A grim line settled on Gavin's lips.

Cora detected his fury bubbling below the surface.

"Originals need neurowalls for our safety," he said in a low, deadly tone. "This armor won't operate with a neurowall, which leaves me vulnerable to people like you."

She sensed his increasing instability.

"By the way, that door won't open," he said with a chuckle. "At least not until I send the correct code sequence."

Cora paused in the middle of the room, wracking her brain for new escape ideas.

"So, you killed Aria first and Drew second," she said, clutching her hands to keep her fingers from trembling. "Is there a significance to the order of the deaths?"

"No, but Drew had to go after he destroyed Trudy's reputation," he said. "You may not know this, but Originals are a bit conservative. They see it as a way of separating themselves from Askovs."

"When you went after Jane, did you cause the fighting in Lunar City?" she asked, stepping away from the door.

"It was too easy," he said with a broad smile. "The casino bosses are constantly at each other's throats. I simply sent several unflattering messages to all of them, knowing at least one would take the bait. It worked better than I'd hoped."

"Porter told me he helped Trudy, but you said you planned to kill him," she said, eyebrows wrinkled in confusion. "Why kill him at all? He seems to be supportive of Originals."

"He killed my family!" he shouted, straightening away from the table.

There it is, she thought, sensing strong currents of his increasing insanity. *I have to get out of here.*

He took a couple of steps toward her and she stepped further into the living room, stopping at the coffee table.

"You seem to want to talk," he said with a smile that had none of his previous charm. "Do you think someone's coming for you? Ferna Robertson, Brian and Benjamin Farris are all busy. I checked."

"How do you plan to kill Linus?" she asked, inching her way toward the end of the coffee table.

"I'm going to torture him first," he chuckled as Cora winced. "He never spent a single day in prison nor a penal colony. Five years' probation was an insult for killing three humans."

"Did you disable Porter's game a few years ago?" she asked, taking a backward step from the coffee table after reaching the end. "He told me an interesting story where his game became infected with a super virus and his game's AI couldn't clean the code. This caused him to purchase a more complex AI to fix his game. After his game was working, Porter was in more debt. Coincidentally, you injected the needed credits, making you a partner."

"You figured it out," he scowled. "I knew you'd be trouble when I first met you. I thought about killing you after I looked into your background. But the rumors seemed exaggerated. Turns out, I really should've killed you."

Cora wracked her mind for a forgotten memory—there was something about her suite. Backup plan? Safety? Portals! Every room had an airlock in case of a sudden decompression in Lunar City. The suite was a separate module that used to be part of a spaceship. The fuel wouldn't let the module lift off from the moon, but it would provide enough emergency energy and food to keep everyone fed and warm for months.

She squinted as a plan formed in her head. Those airlocks worked both ways—they locked air in or let it out. She raced to her bedroom and locked the door, knowing it wouldn't hold long. She guessed Gavin had the code to unlock every door in the building. She found the portal behind a small pastel sofa, opened it, wiggled through the tiny tunnel-like space, locking it behind her. As she shimmied through the dimly lit tunnel, the end widened, revealing a ladder that led to the floor below.

Stale air surrounded her as she stepped on to the ladder at the eleventh floor. The low lighting made it difficult to see the rungs of the ladder initially, but she made it to the tenth floor. She froze when she heard something banging against the airlock in her bedroom. A new frisson of fear raced down her spin, forcing her to increase her steps on the ladder. She had almost reached the ninth floor when she heard steps on the ladder above her.

"I know you're down there Coraline Brimble," Gavin yelled. "I can't have you chasing me—I have more work to do."

Her breathing increased as she climbed down even faster. Her sweaty hands caused her to slip past a few rungs on the ladder. But she managed to catch herself. When she reached the seventh floor, she noticed a button that read 'Seventh Floor Airlock.'

How did I miss that earlier, she thought as sweat ran down the sides of her face?

She pressed the portal button, but nothing happened, and she continued her race to the bottom. Gavin's thuds on the ladder grew closer as she tried entering every apartment on her way down, but they were all locked. Her hands burned with each grip on the rungs, but she couldn't slow down.

On the fourth floor, she pressed the airlock button and heard its distinctive hiss. She could have cried with happiness as she scrambled through the meter long tunnel to the open portal and dropped inside a dark apartment. She locked the hatch, knowing Gavin would be there in a minute or two.

"Lights," Cora asked the suite's AI. Hoping and terrified someone occupied the room. She stood in a silent, inky black room. Since the AI wasn't working, she guessed it must be empty.

Hoping that all the suites comprised the same layout, she stumbled through what she thought was a bedroom, bumping her knees against furniture. She blundered into an unlit room and stuck her hands in front. Picking her way through what she assumed was the living and dining room combination, she reached the entrance to the suite. She heard the distinctive hiss of the airlock behind her and raced through the door.

It didn't open at first as she scratched at the edges, frantic to activate safety features that allowed doors to open to the touch. After what felt like an hour, but was probably only a second or two, the door slid open and she staggered through. She took off running and the door to the suite whooshed closed. When she reached the door to the stairs, it slid open, but she hesitated, realizing Gavin could outrun her. She changed her mind and continued down the hall to the antigrav lift.

She set her mind to another thing she'd remembered from the orientation and activated her comm bracelet. The antigrav lift opened, and she dived in, pressing the emergency button displayed on the floating screen. She turned just in time to lock eyes with Gavin before the doors closed. Gavin would try to override the safety controls, but that would take time. She hoped he wasn't fast enough for the trip to the ground floor.

When the antigrav lift's doors opened again, she dashed out, heading for the exit, but collided with someone.

"Brian," Cora cried.

He held her as she trembled while she tried to suck in huge breaths.

"Cover the airlocks and the stairs," Agent Taylor said in a strong, authoritative voice. Several boots ran to the portal behind a large potted plant and more ran to the stairs.

"Gavin's on the fourth floor," Cora said, out of breath. "He's wearing tactical armor. You won't be able to see him."

"Don't worry, Steven helped us change our scanners so we can see him," Agent Taylor said. "You two have a seat here." She directed Cora and Brian to the nearest bench and stood nearby, issuing orders to the remaining IPS agents.

"Steven contacted me," Brian said, giving her a squeeze. "This time I didn't argue, but raced here as fast as possible. I'm guessing he called Agent Taylor because she arrived just behind me."

They huddled on the bench while Cora's trembling decreased and finally stopped. Half an hour later, they heard thumping and shouting behind the airlock. The first agent stumbled out, followed by Gavin, who was handcuffed.

"You all deserve to die," Gavin screamed several times.

Cora winced, remembering she hadn't raised her shield. It didn't matter earlier because all IPS agents wore neurowalls. But Gavin was actually insane, and his emotional waves hurt like hammers inside her head. After a moment of concentration, she built her shield, and the pain disappeared.

Brian squeezed her, holding her even closer.

CHAPTER 21

Early the next morning, Cora walked with Brian from the IPS headquarters near Brian's office. He held her while she leaned against him as they took a shortcut through Central Park. After a few minutes, the Athos Tower loomed before them.

"I'm so tired, I only want to collapse into bed," Cora said with a yawn. She was still wearing her soft-pink dress, now rumpled. Agent Taylor had brought a human doctor to examine Cora. But she was unharmed—Gavin hadn't laid a hand on her.

"We're almost there," Brian said in a comforting voice. He still wore a casual business suit, which was also wrinkled.

They'd spent the entire evening at the IPS headquarters. Agent Taylor subjected them to several rounds of questions, trying to gather additional evidence against Gavin Smith. Now, they found a small crowd waiting for them in front of Athos Tower, which included Aunt Ferna and Benjamin and a few faces Cora didn't recognize.

"Oh, oh. There they are," Aunt Ferna yelled as she quickened her steps toward Cora and Brian. "Oh my dear, how are you? Did he hurt you?"

"No, aunt, I'm fine," Cora said with a small smile. "I think I just need a good night's sleep. I didn't get to sleep all night with all the questioning."

"Yes, we know all about that," Benjamin said. "The IPS wouldn't let us in last night. It took them all night to remove Gavin's viruses he installed to control all the doors in the building."

Steven must've helped them, Cora thought.

"I don't think you're going to be able to sleep yet," Brian muttered.

"Come here, my dear," Aunt Ferna wrapped an arm around Cora's waist and helped her into the lobby and onto the antigrav lift. "The IPS left and gave us permission to enter thirty minutes before you arrived."

"Did you spend the night outside?" Cora asked, a little alarmed.

"No. I slept at Kenna's home and Benjamin at Omar's," Aunt Ferna said, stepping down the hall and into their suite.

Even though a larger crowd greeted her outside the building, the only people who entered were Brian, Aunt Ferna, Benjamin, and Porter.

Cora wondered why Porter turned up, but she was too tired to start that conversation.

"My dear, tell us what happened last night," Aunt Ferna asked, placing a cup of hot coffee in Cora's hands.

Everyone took a moment to sip on tea or coffee while Brian and Aunt Ferna nibbled on peach and blueberry muffins.

Cora explained how Gavin entered their suite, confessed to killing Aria to upset Linus. He executed Drew because of his treatment of Trudy. He'd planned to kill Jane and then Porter, and he saved Linus for last.

Porter froze with a coffee cup halfway to his mouth. Everyone else at the table peered at him.

"Was he really going to kill me?" Porter asked with eyebrows raised.

Cora nodded.

"I was so frightened," Aunt Ferna said, reaching out to Cora and squeezing her hand. "I always said that coming to Lunar City was a terrible idea. We need to go back home as soon as possible."

Cora and Brian exchanged glances. She'd had too much experience with Aunt Ferna's revisionist memory to even try to argue.

"I only now heard what happened," Porter said in a quiet voice. "Are you alright?"

"Yes," Cora said with a yawn.

"I know you've been awake all night," Porter said. "I wanted to say how embarrassed and sorry I am, especially because I lectured everyone about mistreating Originals."

"Well, it all ended well," Cora said with a sip of coffee.

"You don't understand," Porter said, frowning. "I've known Gavin for three or four years now. I had no idea he was Xavier Varney. He must've suffered so much with the loss of his kids, and I didn't notice how unstable he'd become. I missed all the signs, and it nearly cost you your life."

Cora reached across the table for his hand. He reached out, and they squeezed each other's hands.

"I don't blame you for anything," she said. "Gavin treated you like a son, which must've felt good after your family abandoned you five years ago."

Nobody spoke for a moment.

"To me, the most disturbing thing was the hidden insanity," Cora said with a shudder.

"What will happen to him?" Porter asked.

"According to Agent Taylor, the IPS will turn him over to the EGS," Brian said. "Most of his theft actually happened on Earth, and he stole from the EGS."

"Then he'll disappear," Aunt Ferna said in a flat voice. "That's what the EGS does."

"I'm not sure that's true in this case," Benjamin said. "Gavin is an Original. EGS testing focuses on Askovs. There probably aren't any tests for Originals."

"I wouldn't be too sure," Aunt Ferna said, pushing her empty plate away. "When they create new gadgets to protect Originals, somebody has to be the first person to try them out."

"Original or Askov. It doesn't matter to me," Benjamin said in a firm voice. "A murderer still needs to go to prison or a penal colony."

"Speaking of killers, Hilda was right," Aunt Ferna said, turning away from Benjamin. They never agreed on that topic because of the EGS's treatment of Oliver. "You should thank Hilda for saving your life. She predicted you'd be safe as long as you weren't alone." She grinned.

"I don't see it that way," Cora said, stifling a yawn. "What she really said was: 'as long as she's never alone outside of her suite, she'll be safe.' I was alone inside the suite, and Gavin strolled in."

"Before Gavin entered, you were alone," Aunt Ferna said with a raised eyebrow. "Did he harm you? No. You don't have a scratch on you."

Cora glowered at her and thought about trying to argue, but she was too tired. Aunt Ferna usually dodged her logic anyway.

"Maybe we should continue this conversation a little later," Brian said.

"Now consider the reverse of Hilda's statement," Aunt Ferna continued, as if Brian hadn't spoken. "When Gavin arrived in the suite, you were in danger. All you had to do was exit the suite, which you did. You were always safe, my dear."

Cora sighed, feeling the heaviness of her eyes and limbs overriding her ability to think.

"Come along," Brian said as he helped Cora to her feet and turned to everybody else. "Good morning." He helped her to her room and tucked her into bed.

In the middle of the afternoon, Cora woke with a start. She'd had a dream about Gavin chasing her round the dining room table. He nearly caught her when she woke up. Her hands ached from holding on to the ladder yesterday. The doctor had warned her of a few aches and pains after the physical exertion, but felt it was better to let her body heal itself.

She rolled out of bed and stumbled to the bathroom. She showered and changed to an azure top with matching pants. Her stomach rumbled, and she made her way to the dining room.

"Afternoon, sleepyhead," Brian said with a bright smile. He sat with a plate of toast with scrambled synthetic eggs and a cup of coffee.

"That looks good," Cora said, taking a seat next to him. "I'll have the same." She made her selection in the meal crafter.

She bit into a crunchy piece of toast topped with soft-scrambled eggs. The combination of hard-and-crunchy blending with soft-and-salty creating a comforting yet savory breakfast classic.

"Better?" he asked.

"Yeah," she said, swallowing some coffee. "I didn't realize how hungry I was."

"Me too," he said, reaching for his cup. "This is my second breakfast."

They chuckled.

"Do you have plans today?" she asked.

"Canceled," he said. "I feel like I need to protect you for at least a little while."

Cora nodded.

"Wait. I hope you don't have plans," he said with furrowed eyebrows.

"No." She chuckled. "It's just... When Gavin tried to kill me, I was terrified. The only other time I've been that scared was when Oliver tried to kill me. Both times I thought I might actually die..." She paused, gathering her thoughts. "This time it hit me. I didn't want to die without telling you I love you."

Brian put his cup down, reached for her, and hugged her. He kissed both of her cheeks.

"I don't know why I couldn't say it earlier," she said. "I could blame my emotionally distant parents, vile sister, or evil cousin. But really, I was just so scared."

"What's so scary about I love you?" he asked with a gentle squeeze.

"I don't know," she said and paused for a moment. "Before Aunt Ferna came into my life, family meant pain. It was mostly emotional, but sometimes physical. With her I learned to love and I thought I was over that part of my life."

"Well, I love you too," he said with a gentle kiss on her mouth.

"My life wouldn't be complete without you," Cora said as a light happiness settled in her chest.

***

To enjoy more cozy mystery science fiction, pick up Spencer Legacy (https://katherinesb ooks.com/spencerlegacy/).

Please Leave an Honest Review

Authors thrive on reviews. These reviews help other readers decide whether to buy the book. To write a review, simply go back to the website where you purchased this book, provide a star rating, and add a couple of sentences explaining why you liked the book. Thank you for your review.

Review Link (https://katherinesbooks.com/lunar-review)

WOULD YOU LIKE ANOTHER SCI-FI WHODUNIT?

Want to know how it all began? Dive into *Short Stories from the Feeler Universe* (https://katherinesbooks.com/sci-fi-short-story/), and once you join my newsletter, read this thrilling short story from *The Feeler* series! This prequel takes you to the very beginning, where Cora uses her unique Feeler abilities to unravel a gripping whodunit.

BOOKS

Standalone Books

The Puzzle Safe Mystery
https://katherinesbooks.com/psmamz
The Runaway Martian
https://katherinesbooks.com/runawaymartia
namz
***

The Feeler Series Books

The Feeler (Book 1)
katherinesbooks.com/feeler
Movers, Mines, and Murder (Book 2)
katherinesbooks.com/movers
Lunar Justice (Book 3)
katherinesbooks.com/lunarjustice
Spencer Legacy (Book 4)

katherinesbooks.com/spencerlegacy

About the
Author

Katherine is a science fiction author who spent nearly thirty years working as an engineer before retiring and turning to her life-long love of storytelling. She grew up devouring classic sci-fi, especially the works of Isaac Asimov, Arthur C. Clarke, and Ray Bradbury. As much as she adored those stories, she often felt something was missing.

Over time, her reading tastes broadened to include cozy mysteries, thrillers, and fantasy. Eventually she realized her ideal book would be a blend of the genres she loved most. The solution was obvious: write cross-genre stories that fuse the wonder of science fiction with the charm and puzzle-solving of cozy mystery.

Katherine lives in New England, where she spends her days writing, reading, and enjoying time with her family.

www.ingramcontent.com/pod-product-compliance
Lightning Source LLC
Chambersburg PA
CBHW051330020726
47501CB00007B/2005